### Demon's Lair

There was no time to think.

They were staring into a gaping black hole in the ground. The next moment something was climbing out, swiftly, effortlessly, and then it was standing on the trail. Jennifer screamed when the wolf creature slammed into her, and the club flew from her hand as she fell. The impact knocked the air from her lungs, and she gasped, tears filling her eyes while the alien tried to get its hands around her throat. She thrashed and tried to yell, but the thing was too strong. . . .

Most iBooks are available at special quantity discounts for bulk purchases for sales promotions, premiums or fundraising. Special books or book excerpts can also be created to fit specific needs.
For details, email the publisher
@bricktower@aol.com

# PRIVATE
# SCHOOL
## #3

# WITCH'S EYE

### Steven Charles

A BYRON PREISS VISUAL PUBLICATIONS, INC.
BOOK

iBooks for Young Readers
Habent Sua Fata Libelli

**iBooks**
Manhanset House
Dering Harbor, New York 11965

bricktower@aol.com • www.ibooksinc.com

Library of Congress Cataloging-in-Publication Data
Charles, Steven. Witch's eye.
    (Private School) "A Byron Preiss book."
p. cm.
    [1. Young Adult Fiction—Horror. 2. Young Adult Fiction—Science
Fiction—Alien Contact. 3. Young Adult Fiction—Werewolfs and
        Shifters.] I. Lang, Gary, iII. II. Title. III.
        Series: Charles, Steven. Private School.

ISBN 978-1-59687-732-0
December 2018

SPECIAL THANKS TO RON BUEHL,
PAT MACDONALD, MARJORIE HANLON,
AND DAVID M. HARRIS.
EDITOR—RUTH ASHBY

# WITCH'S EYE

# Table of Contents

# One

JENNIFER KNEW SHE WAS GOING TO DIE.

There was no question about it.

*They're watching you, girl.*

Something out there was watching.

Out there in back, where the hills and forest stopped and the rich lawn of the campus began, something in the dark. Unseen by the stars, untouched by the moon.

Watching. Waiting. As it had been for days.

With the patience of an animal stalking its prey.

Jennifer turned away from her dormitory window with a shudder and returned to the mirror over her dresser.

Something. Someone. Watching.

She shook her head sharply.

*They're watching you all.*

She shook her head again, took a deep breath, and deliberately slammed her brush onto the dresser top, driving the voices away.

"That's it," she declared. An auburn lock of hair drooped over her forehead. She glared at it in the mirror, blew it back into place, and when it fell back over her brow, she said again, "That's it, I give up."

A barely smothered giggle spun Jennifer around, and she scowled at the black-haired girl sitting on the edge of the bed.

1

"What do you think you're laughing at, Beauford?" she demanded. "We have a crisis here, can't you see that?"

Marysue Beauford pushed herself to her feet with a gentle shake of her head. She could not keep her voice, deep and soft and touched with a gentle Virginia accent, from sounding as if she were ready to break into laughter.

"Field, in the first place, we don't have a lot of choice, remember?"

"Yes, but—"

"And in the second place, don't interrupt. Turn around and let me at that rat's nest you call hair."

Jennifer did, but her reflection looked no better. Her hair was too long, her face was flushed, the tilt of her nose made her look like Bob Hope. And the soft white blouse Marysue had lent her exposed more of her than would be revealed in a bathing suit—it was much too clinging, much too transparent, and if her father could have seen her then, he would have thrown her out of their house.

"I can't do it," she said miserably.

"For heaven's sake, girl, will you stop complaining? You act like you've never done this before."

"I haven't."

Marysue looked heavenward. "Oh, lord, spare me this, please, and I'll never cut class again."

"But don't you understand? This isn't like we're going to the movies, Beauford. We're talking major humiliation here. People are actually going to *see* me. This is going to be a disaster."

"You want disaster?" Marysue said. "Wait until you see what old Mrs. Klopher looks like when she thinks she's dressed up. She looks like the Phantom of the Opera in drag."

Jennifer tried to imagine the academy's head librarian in a long black cloak and monster makeup. "I'm gonna look like her," she decided glumly. "Nobody's going to be able to tell us apart."

A sharp yank of the brush made her yelp and finally laugh. But she didn't protest again.

Mixers, she thought sourly. Bus in some boys from other private schools, let them all crowd into the gym, stand against the walls, and stare at one another while an amateur band blares too loudly for anyone to talk without shouting. Mixers. At home they were simply called dances, and at home she would have known practically everyone who'd be there.

But at Thaler Academy there were no boys who lived on campus. And those who'd be there that night she would probably never see again. So why bother?

Because it was The Rule. The dean had said there would be a dance; he said all students would attend, and the only exceptions were for those who were off campus on field trips.

Marysue drew the brush down one more time, tilted her head, and nodded her satisfaction. "You are ready, Ms. Field."

"No, I'm not."

But she stood back from the dresser, turned, and looked over her shoulder. Actually, she admitted after a moment's inspection, she really didn't look too bad. A little rich looking in Marysue's clothes for her taste. But she hadn't brought anything fancy with her and didn't have the money to go into town and buy something new for the occasion. So, all things considered, she supposed she looked all right.

If only so much didn't *show*.

Then she saw Marysue grinning. "What?" she demanded.

"I was just thinking about poor old Lee. If he ever sees you looking this way, he's going to have a cardiac on the spot."

Jennifer felt a blush rise to her cheeks and turned away quickly before her friend could spot it. If only Lee were there, she wouldn't feel quite so out of place. The boys coming from the other schools were much like Marysue—well-off and virtually assured of places in Ivy League colleges once their exclusive secondary education was done. Lee Fawkes, on the other hand, was the son of a hardware store owner in Staines, the town closest to Thaler; he took a couple of courses at the academy because he was bright, but he seldom came to any of the functions because he, like she, felt as if he didn't belong.

The difference between them was that she didn't have a chip on her shoulder. Lee sneered at the rich Thaler students because he refused to admit that, despite their wealth, they could be as human as he was.

He did like Marysue and thought she was an exception, but still he argued with her now and then and made remarks that caused her to snap back at him.

Lee, Jennifer thought fondly, you really can be a trial sometimes.

But she still wished he would come.

Finally, after fussing with her neckline again and pushing at her hair with a silent, helpless sigh, she decided she couldn't stall any longer. She looked glumly around the dormitory room, as if she'd never see it again, and slowly opened the door. A cacophony of sound instantly washed over her from girls racing along the green-tiled hall shouting for assistance, from their high-pitched laughter, and from their heels on the stairs that led down to the first floor.

Except for the clothes, it might have been a normal evening at Thaler.

And then the thought struck her with the force of a physical blow: *Nothing would ever be normal at Thaler again. Nothing would ever be normal anywhere again.*

Nothing.

And the voices returned: *They know, they know you all.*

With a shudder she glanced over her shoulder and saw Marysue standing unmoving in the center of the room. Her hands were clasped tightly in front of her, her expression that of one walking into a dark room, knowing that someone is in there, someone who wants to do her harm.

Jennifer knew then that Marysue heard voices of her own.

"Field," Marysue finally said, shaking her head and moving toward the door. "Are you going to stand around all night or what?"

Jennifer looked up, and when Marysue gave her a playful shove she even managed a smile as they hurried out the door, down the stairs, and out the dorm's front door.

"Beautiful," Marysue said, taking a deep breath.

"Cold," Jennifer muttered.

Beauford laughed and took her friend's arm, and together they hurried along the covered porches and walkways that linked the campus's main buildings. At the last one, a well-lighted dormitory from which music and laughter exploded, they turned onto a path that led down a gentle slope to the gymnasium, where the mixer was being held.

The lights from the dorm soon faded, the lights from the gymnasium were too far away, and the moonlight served only to add shadows to the lawn, to make the hills and trees behind the school darker and more forbidding.

Jennifer looked from side to side nervously, stumbled once over nothing, and caught her breath when a dark figure burst out of the night and raced past them. A girl, Jen, she told herself angrily; it's only a girl, that's all. Calm down.

The nightwind rose.

A fragment of cloud drifted across the moon.

Marysue was humming softly, her head tilted as if listening for other sounds.

Jennifer slowed.

Something was out there.

Music from the gym blared momentarily when a door was opened, light spilled onto the grass, and there was the sound of hard-driving drums and high laughter.

Something . . .

The door closed again, the light and the noise were cut off, and Jennifer stopped, arms rigid at her sides.

There, between the crescent of buildings and the first of the trees, something was standing on the lawn, just out of reach of the light.

Watching her. Watching Marysue.

She blinked, telling herself it was only the shadow from a tree or a piece of equipment left out on the grass.

Nerves. Only her nerves.

It moved.

At first she thought it was just the wind causing the shadow of a branch to shift, but when the figure moved again she knew nerves had nothing to do with it.

Marysue had walked on several yards, stopping at last when she realized she was alone. She looked over her shoulder at Jennifer beckoning urgently.

"What?" she asked, taking her time getting back.

Jennifer pointed.

It moved again, closer to the trees, almost blending now with the forest's dark wall.

Marysue leaned over and stared. "What am I looking at?"

"There!" she insisted, jabbing her finger at the place where the figure had stood.

And watched.

Marysue stopped, and her eyes narrowed. "Wait a minute. Are you telling me—"

"It's there!" she said, taking a step off the walk. "I can see it as clearly as I can see you. It's standing—" And her shoulders slumped, her arm lowered.

It was gone.

The night had drawn it in, and it was gone.

"But I saw it," she said, not following as Beauford started for the gym again.

For a moment Jennifer thought Marysue was going to leave her there, but Marysue took only a few steps before turning slowly and returning.

She glanced to her right.

"You did see it?"

Jennifer nodded.

"It was one of them?"

She nodded again, then shook her head. "I think so," she said.

They stood together, shivering, paying no attention now to the occasional music or the lights. A group of girls chattering loudly passed them and moved toward the gym; but they saw only the dark, and Jennifer sensed again a watching in the shadows and knew that whatever moved among the trees was not her imagination.

"I don't feel like dancing," Marysue said in a small voice that carried none of her usual strut and style.

"Me neither."

A harsh wind gusted out of the hills, blowing their hair into their eyes, filling their ears with the sounds of rattling branches, the snakelike hiss of rustling leaves.

They didn't look at each other.

They ran.

# Two

THERE WAS ONLY A HANDFUL OF GIRLS IN THE DORM'S first-floor common room when Jennifer and Marysue charged through the doors. Startled, they looked up at the noise, but Jennifer only grinned at them, gave them a wave and a quick comment about the cold weather, and followed Marysue up the stairs as fast as she could without running.

Once back in her room, she switched on the overhead light and the desk lamp and stood at the window, seeing her reflection and the dark night beyond. Then, in a single move, she pulled the curtains closed and turned around.

Marysue was still at the door, leaning against it, rubbing her arms to bring back the warmth.

It isn't going to end, Jennifer thought.

The nightmare had been born out of innocent curiosity.

Jennifer, Marysue, and their friend Monica Holt had stumbled upon a secret, working laboratory in a supposedly abandoned science building in the woods behind the campus. While the other girls thought they ought to forget it, Jennifer had been curious. She wanted to know what was going on, why anyone would want to hide a lab. Despite the others' warnings of dire consequences should the dean find out, Jennifer had explored.

And in the exploring she had uncovered the nightmare—the lab didn't house anything like a government-sponsored project, or even a private one run by one of the school's science instructors.

The lab was, they had learned to their horror, the base—perhaps one of many—of wolflike creatures who were able to disguise themselves almost perfectly as humans and who used hidden life-support systems to enable them to walk around unnoticed.

Creatures, they soon learned, who were from out there, beyond the stars.

At first Jennifer had believed there was only a handful, attached to the academy by some unknown link.

Now she knew there were more.

"The dean," Marysue said then, her face a bit pale though her cheeks were still flushed from running.

"What about him?" Jennifer answered, flopping onto the bed and kicking off her good shoes.

"He's gonna kill us for not going."

She looked up and sighed. "Marysue," she said patiently, "there are a zillion people on campus tonight. Do you think he's really going to know which two of them—us—aren't at the gym?"

"But what if he does?"

Despite the scare they'd just had, Jennifer almost laughed. "For crying out loud, we've changed places. You've always broken every rule at Thaler, and *now* you're afraid the dean'll find out we didn't go."

"Yeah, well, I'm learning discretion from you, child, and you know the dean."

Although she knew her friend was talking about Dean Dramon's famous temper when his rules were not obeyed, she also knew there was something more at stake.

Peter Dramon was an extremely handsome man in a dangerously dark sort of way. His elegance was apparent, and his appeal to the women clear.

But his dark eyes often put the lie to the frequent smiles on his lips—his eyes were cold and flat with just a flicker of menace, which Jennifer couldn't swear was really there but saw just the same whenever she was with him.

Marysue and her boy friend, Conrad Chang, believed he couldn't really be one of the wolf-creatures because of his position—he had too many connections and dealings with the outside world.

But Jennifer thought he had to be one. Or at least on their side.

Jennifer and her friends had discovered that the board of trustees that supposedly administered Thaler Academy did not exist any longer. The school and all its property had been purchased slowly by Dramon, and Dramon alone during his ten years on the board of trustees. And it was at Thaler that the aliens had begun whatever work they were doing, setting in motion whatever plan it was that had brought them there in the first place.

As she unbuttoned her blouse she pointed at the door. "Don't worry about him," she said. "We'll cross that bridge when we come to it. Right now, we're safer in the dorm, and we're going to stay here. Why don't you go get changed and meet me back here. Then we'll decide what to do next."

"Oh, great," Marysue said. "All of a sudden you're filled with ideas. And it was your ideas that got us into this in the first place."

Muttering, she left with her head down. Jennifer changed quickly into jeans and a blouse and sweater. She knew what her friend was thinking and how frustrated she was becoming.

She remembered a night only six days before that now seemed like a hundred, when she had stood in the dorm hall and watched other girls opening the doors to their rooms and stepping into the hall. One by one. Staring at her. Blankly. And she could have sworn that each of them had green, glowing eyes.

The moment had passed as quickly as it had come, but she couldn't forget it. And it had confirmed what one of the aliens had implied to her just before he died—that he wasn't the only one left.

If her life had been a nightmare before, that night it became a sentence in a dungeon cell. She felt trapped, knowing she had jailers and not knowing precisely who any of them were. She had her suspicions, but no way to prove them. And the worst part of it was going through each day as if nothing was wrong, as if she knew nothing, had seen nothing, was nothing more than an ordinary student whose classes and studies took up most of her time.

She had to keep up the pretense, not just to maintain her sanity, but also to stop her parents from finding out something was wrong.

Marysue came in then without knocking, grinned, and flopped into one of the room's two armchairs. She pulled at the bottom of her white ski sweater and sniffed. "So," she said, "how are you going to save the world?"

Jennifer squeezed between her and the desk to face the casement window overlooking the dark hills behind the campus. The wind had come up, hissing out of the trees to slap against the panes. A draft found the gap between window frame and wall, and she shivered as she watched the moon lay a path of silver across the lawn below.

No shadows now, nothing watching, and she hitched herself up onto the broad sill. But before she was settled, there was a knock on the door. She stared across the room, looked at Marysue, and frowned.

Another knock, more insistent.

And she suddenly became angry that now she was even afraid of someone at her door. "Come in!" she called, and Monica Holt walked in. She was wearing a sweater and designer jeans, and her face was still pale from her recent surgery. She posed for a moment in the doorway, fluffing at long brown hair that fell in cascades to her shoulders. "You like?" she asked.

Marysue groaned dramatically. "It's just horrible."

Monica looked at Jennifer, who took in the wig, the face, and finally giggled. "Horrible," she said, "isn't strong enough."

The girl sighed and yanked the hair off. "I know. I keep trying, though. I've got four now, and they all make me look like I'm wearing a wig." Her natural hair, a close-cropped blond, was slightly mussed, and she swiped at it with both hands as she dropped onto the bed and sat with her back against the wall. "Aren't you going to the mixer?"

"Are you kidding?" Marysue said. "I can hear the music from here, thank you very much. I think my ears would be safer listening to dear Esther Fine singing in the shower."

Monica laughed, tilting her head forward. "Not nice, Beauford. Remember, we're supposed to set an example for Field here. You wouldn't want her to think badly of us Thaler girls, would you?"

Jennifer grinned, pleased that Holt was regaining her familiar, sometimes biting sense of humor after suffering an illness she had kept from everyone until its course had been resolved.

"My, it's getting cold!" Marysue exclaimed with a look at the window to see if it was open. "My dears, I shall perish if they don't move this whole school to Florida right this minute."

Jennifer felt the cold as well, but, even more, she felt the shame surging again, the shame that came when she had accused Monica of being an alien. As it turned out, she couldn't have been more wrong. And once apologies had been made and explanations given, Monica had surprised them all with her generous forgiveness.

"How are you feeling?" Jennifer said when Holt finally stopped laughing.

The girl shrugged and touched her side gingerly. "All this time and it still smarts."

"We saw something tonight," Marysue said abruptly.

Monica looked at her strangely. "You did? Really?"

Jennifer nodded and told her about the figure she had spotted watching her and of the feelings she had had all week.

Monica nodded without saying a word, and Jennifer said, "I'm not putting up with this anymore." Her hands bunched into fists. "I mean, we've got to do something. I can't go around being afraid of my own shadow all the time."

The cold intensified, and Jennifer kicked at the radiator's metal covering beneath her legs, jumped off the sill, and groaned when she realized she hadn't turned the heat on. Marysue raised a mocking fist, and Monica suggested they go down to the common room where at least they wouldn't freeze to death.

The study room to the left of the foyer was dark, and the common room was empty. After a few seconds of aimless wandering they sprawled on one of the couches, facing the high front windows. There was a silence in the room that told them the building was deserted, a faint rumbling in the furnace, a creak of a floorboard, the muffled cry of the wind.

"Friday night and no place to go," Monica said quietly.

Jennifer watched their reflections in the dark glass, the three of them each wearing at least once piece of white, like three ghosts viewed through a sheet of black ice. She shivered and tightened her lips.

Marysue shifted around, looking for a more comfortable position, and suddenly stood straight up.

"An idea?" Jennifer asked.

"No," Marysue whispered. "Don't you hear it?"

The trio was silent for a while, straining to hear and then to identify the faint sound in the distance.

"Footsteps. That's what it is, footsteps," Marysue exclaimed.

Jennifer concentrated on the distant noise. "No," she decided. "The rhythm is wrong for someone walking."

"It's footsteps. I'm positive. It sounds like someone snooping around. And I'm going to find out who it is." Marysue rose and walked to the door. "Are you two coming?"

Monica and Jennifer looked at each other and shrugged. "At least it's something positive to do," Jennifer said.

The sound echoed faintly through the foyer, irregularly, like a tree tapping a window in the wind, but so diffused by the echoes that the source remained a mystery. They circled cautiously, trying to pin the sound down, but the reverberations baffled them.

Jennifer said, "I'll check upstairs. You two can argue about who looks in the study room." Without waiting for them, she headed up the stairs.

Reminding herself that she had volunteered out of curiosity, not fear, Jennifer looked carefully down to both ends of the corridor at the top of the stairs. Empty. So if it was a prowler, he wouldn't be jumping out behind her. The sound was a little louder up there than it had been downstairs.

Slowly and as quietly as she was able, she crept down the corridor on her right. Blocks of wall broken only by closed and locked doors marked her way with no interruption. The echoes there were as bad as those in the foyer, and she couldn't tell whether she was getting closer to or farther away from the source of the sound.

Turning the corner, Jennifer could momentarily hear voices from below. Beauford and Holt squabbling again, she thought. How could they ever hope to find a noise if they made so much themselves? But with the voices fading behind her, the dormitory settled once more into silence.

The silence of complete abandonment.

Except for the soft but now steady tapping somewhere ahead of her.

It was unnerving, and Jennifer had a moment of panic. Until then the dorm had been her refuge, her place of safety; she had thought the aliens would never reveal themselves there. Had she been too confident? Jennifer looked back over her shoulder down the hallway she had just walked. Still empty.

The footsteps were even louder then. She was thinking of the noise as footsteps now, she realized. She was assuming that someone was prowling, someone who had no kindly intentions toward her. And the sound was at its loudest just there, just then—as she stood before her own door.

There's no way, she told herself, that there's an alien in there. It's not possible. She repeated it until she had almost convinced herself that it was true.

She threw her door open.

The radiator. The radiator was loudly protesting its having to function again. With a silent laugh at herself, Jennifer went back to the top of the stairs and leaned over the railing, shouting down, "I found it. It's the heat coming up in my room, and my radiator's knocking."

She waited, still leaning against the balustrade, looking down to the floor below for her friends. Their friendly bickering told her they were coming.

And suddenly she was pitched forward! Just managing to shift her weight and thrust herself sideways so she didn't fall headfirst over the railing and onto the floor one story below.

She started to tumble down the staircase, over and over, her body coiled tight, her arms protecting her head.

Her headlong flight stopped as she barreled into her two friends on the central landing. The girls were sufficiently braced to stop them all from continuing to fall down the remaining stairs. They caught their breath as they lay in a shaken heap.

Monica pulled herself out of the tangle of limbs, holding her side while trying to catch her breath. "I know you're glad to see us," she said, "but this is ridiculous."

Jennifer finished checking herself for broken bones. Finding none, she said, "I was tripped."

"You mean you fell," said Marysue, finally standing.

"No," Jennifer insisted. "I was tripped. Well, anyway, something—or someone—knocked my feet out from under me."

"You said that it was the radiator. Now you say someone's up there. Make up your mind, girl." Marysue sighed with mock exasperation.

Jennifer spoke slowly, not wanting to lose the thread. "The noise was the radiator. You can still hear it. But I *was* tripped. I felt something against my legs, and then

I was falling. I'm certain of it," she said. "Well, almost certain." Could she have imagined it? Could she have gotten dizzy and tripped over her own feet?

"We had better check this out. Field's nerves are unwinding," said Marysue.

Monica and Marysue went back to the top of the stairs and looked around with exaggerated care. "Looks safe so far," Monica said. "But we'd better check out the killer radiator."

Jennifer followed slowly behind them to her room. They were already seated in the two chairs, discussing how the radiator could have pushed her down the stairs, when she entered. Everything was perfectly normal, everything in its place.

But, no, something was wrong.

Something had been moved.

What was it?

Ignoring her friends' chatter, she examined the room. On the desk, everything was as carefully organized as she had left it. Almost everything else she owned was put away, except the brush Marysue had used to fix Jennifer's hair.

"Beauford, where did you leave the brush?"

"Right there, on the dresser."

"Didn't you put it down on the other side?"

Marysue looked at the dresser, trying to remember an insignificant detail. "I have no idea."

"I'm sure you did." Monica looked at Jennifer as though she were catching on, but Jennifer said it anyway. "Someone was in here. I can't prove it, but I'm certain of it."

The three looked at one another for a moment in silence.

Then Marysue shifted uneasily. "Ladies?"

Monica grunted.

"I think we ought to get out of here."

Marysue had called Conrad then and they agreed that he would contact Lee and meet them in the town park near the police station. As soon as that was done, Monica couldn't wait to get off campus. The other two girls barely had time to grab their jackets before Monica pulled out of the student parking lot and they were on their way.

The park was surrounded by a wall of high, trimmed hedges, and Monica stopped her Mercedes at the curb in front of one of the gateless entrances.

"Okay, ladies," Marysue said. "Let's get a move on."

Monica grumbled something about having joined the army, but she slid out.

Jennifer ignored them. They were always arguing about one thing or another, and she had grown used to it. Instead, she jammed her hands into her jacket pockets and hurried into the park, along the path that led toward its center.

Her footsteps were loud, crisp, sounding as if she were walking on thin glass; her breath plumed like faint smoke in front of her, sweeping back into her face and making her shiver; and on either side she could see nothing but black.

The town was cut off in there, and the glow from the occasional white-globed light made it seem as if they were walking through a tunnel.

Marysue whistled but stopped when the notes echoed.

Monica tried humming and stopped just as quickly.

We should have gone to the Hilltop, Jennifer thought as a chill ran through her again. At least there they would have been warm. But Marysue had vetoed the diner; she wanted a place where they could be sure they wouldn't be overheard. Conrad's mom was entertaining, and Lee's mother was still recovering from her recent illness.

So that left the park.

Dead, dry leaves were scattered ahead of them, whispering as they moved through them, snapping under their feet.

The world seemed empty, as if they were the only remaining people.

Finally they reached the playing field in the park's center and followed the path around it until they saw the two boys getting up from a bench on the left.

Lee was bundled in a dark leather jacket with a black fur collar, making him look much larger than he was. His sandy hair was wind tossed, his cheeks red. And when Jennifer hurried up to him, she could see that his dark eyes were narrowed in question.

"Hi," she said.

He grinned. "Hi. You like refrigerators, huh?"

And before she could stop him, he leaned closer and kissed her cheek, took her hand, and held it close to his side.

Conrad Chang was tall and blond, though his somewhat darker skin and slightly tilted eyes made it clear that he favored his Oriental grandfather. His combined heritage made him look exotic, his size made him look like a football player, but his manner was that of a shy little boy who couldn't believe that someone like Marysue could be genuinely interested in someone like him.

"You're gonna catch pneumonia, Zucco," she said, using his nickname, the name of a favorite old-time movie actor who specialized in playing villains and mad scientists. "Does your mother know you're out practically naked?"

He shrugged. He was wearing only a light sweater, and his jeans looked too thin to keep anything warm. "I was in a hurry, remember? I got these orders, see—"

She laughed and put a hand to his mouth to silence him just as Monica came up.

"All right, all right," she said briskly, rubbing her gloved hands together. "Let's get this show on the road, Marysue."

"It's your show," Lee said with a puzzled look at Jennifer. "What's going on?"

"I have an idea how to get us out of this mess, Marysue said."

# Three

BEFORE MARYSUE STARTED TO EXPLAIN, SHE suggested they walk. She didn't want them complaining about the cold while she was talking.

No one objected, and they formed a tight group as they headed past the field, heads down, automatically walking quietly as if afraid they'd be heard.

"All right," she said at last. "The problem is—how do we get people, any people, to believe us? How do we get someone who counts to listen and not think it's a bunch of kids pulling a stupid joke, right? Well, what we have to do is find an alien and capture him." She smiled broadly. "I mean, how simple can it be?"

Jennifer sighed. "Marysue, we already knew we had to do something like that. That's not news, you know."

"Yeah," Beauford said, "but you don't know how, right?"

"Right."

They were interrupted by a distant sound, soft and low when it first reached their ears, louder and higher then until it fell quickly to silence again.

Marysue looked off across the park in the direction of the sound. "That wasn't a siren, was it?"

"Staines doesn't have sirens like that," Conrad told her. "That was an animal."

23

A deep chill walked down Jennifer's back. "I've heard that sound before—something like it."

"A dog. It has to be a dog," Holt decided.

"I just don't know," said Jennifer.

There was a shaking in the bushes not far away, a shaking too violent for the gentle wind that was blowing, and without discussing it the group quickly moved away.

Again the howl pierced the wind.

Walking steadily but slowly next to Lee, Jennifer tried not to show fear. The last time she had heard howling was more than a month before. She wanted Holt to be right. She wanted it to a dog, but couldn't make herself believe it. But no one knew they were in the park; no one had followed the car from the campus; the aliens couldn't have followed them there.

A sound of running feet was coming toward them, and they turned as a group to face the danger. A nearby hedge exploded in motion, and a black beast stormed at them but stopped suddenly just a few feet short of them and howled again.

"That's gotta be the biggest dog I've ever seen," said Lee, laughing.

Marysue moved gingerly up to it, a hand outstretched. "Here, boy. Come to mama." To her friends, she explained, "It's a mastiff. One of our neighbors keeps them. Nice dogs."

The mastiff glared at Marysue, took a step forward, licked her hand, sniffed, and charged off in search of some invisible prey.

The five students laughed in relief and moved on down the path. "I believe, Marysue, you were going to explain how to capture an alien," Conrad said.

"I am."

Marysue had walked on several steps before she realized the others had stopped and were staring at her. "What's the matter?"

Lee hunched his shoulders against a gust of cold wind. "Look," he said, "we've been over this a hundred times and—"

"And nothing," Marysue said smugly. She hurried back and held up her hands. "The trouble is, you've been trying to figure out how to catch one in its natural form. And it can't be done. It's not going to walk up to you, pull off a mask, and say, 'Surprise, sucker!' "

Lee looked away, looked back. "Okay. So—"

"So we have to do it another way. We have to catch one in its human disguise, and I know how to do it."

"Magic," Monica said sarcastically.

"No," said Marysue, suddenly falling against Jennifer. She hit her hard in the side with an elbow, making Jennifer cry out and spin around as if she were going to hit her.

Marysue only grinned and spread her hands. "See?"

Lee shook his head. "No," he said.

"Boy, have I been dumb," Conrad said with a nod.

They had been torn by fear and looked for the most devious method to unmask the intruders, and all the time the answer had been easy—the aliens, as Conrad had figured out, wore something like medicinal patches on their sides, which somehow transformed the atmosphere they were breathing into the atmosphere they needed. What that was they hadn't yet learned.

"Will someone please tell me what you've all figured out?" Lee asked.

"So," Monica said. "What Marysue's saying is that we start hitting people in their sides to see if they fall over, which will probably get us killed."

Marysue groaned, but Jennifer grabbed Monica's sleeve. "No, don't be silly. Think, Monica! How many times are there a bunch of us together, when we could accidentally on purpose collide with someone? It wouldn't have to be obvious. We're not saying you'd have to carry a baseball bat around."

Monica looked doubtful.

Conrad suddenly snapped his fingers. "Gym!" he said.

"Perfect," Lee told him. He looked at Jennifer. "You guys have to take gym three times a week, okay? So you've got all kinds of chances."

All of them began talking at once, throwing out ideas for places where they could use the tactic without appearing as if they had suddenly gone crazy. And as they did, Jennifer backed away slowly, the initial rush of excitement fading when she realized there was a flaw in the plan. More than one, though the others were only vague and disturbing suspicions.

Finally the rest of the group noticed she wasn't talking, and Lee came to her side. "What's the matter?" he asked.

"They'll know what we're doing," she said. "They'll know."

"They know anyway."

She waited until Conrad and the others joined her. "But even if it works, then what? We get one, and the others will—"

"Right," Conrad said. "We can't do it until . . . you know, we can't do it until we get an adult on our side."

"Someone who counts," Lee agreed.

They fell silent for a long moment, turning in small circles in frustration until Monica clapped her hands.

"It can't be just anyone," she said. "Right? It has to be someone who will understand what we're trying to do, and will be able to explain it to the authorities."

Lee shifted. "Yeah, so?"

"Borden Overbrook," Monica said, triumph in her voice. "He's a scientist. He's not attached to the school, not really, he's a visiting lecturer from some big college. If we can get him to see one of these things—"

"Y'know," Marysue said, "I think Holt's got it. He'd be perfect!" Her brow creased in a frown. "But how can we get him to the right place at the right time?"

Lee looked up. "But we all have him in a class. All we have to do is get one while he's in the room. Just one."

Jennifer took his hand then as the others agreed; she took his hand and she squeezed it.

Oh, no, she thought fearfully. Oh, no, it's starting.

The weekend passed slowly.

It was essential, they had decided, to behave as if nothing was wrong, but by Sunday evening Jennifer was ready to scream.

She was in the library on the second floor of the Student Union building. An ecology text was open on the table in front of her, but the words meant nothing, the maps nothing but squiggles, and every time someone walked in and had a word with the student librarian at the front desk, she nearly jumped out of her seat.

"Acid rain," she muttered when she tried to read the page again. "Who cares?"

She wanted to talk to Lee, but he had worked all weekend at his father's store; she wanted to talk to her father, to tell him everything, but Monica had convinced her that he wouldn't believe her. She wanted to go home, but knew that was impossible—she had a responsibility now, one she didn't want and could not be rid of.

She sighed loudly and leaned back, raked her fingers through her hair, and felt the first rumblings of hunger in her stomach. A glance at her watch told her it was after five. With a sigh she gathered her books and made her way toward the exit.

"Hey, Jen?"

She looked at the horseshoe-shaped desk and the chubby girl behind it. "Hi, Es, what's up?"

Esther Fine, wide-eyed in round glasses, her dark hair pulled tightly around her skull, held up an envelope. "This is for you."

Jennifer frowned as she took it. "Who's it from?" she asked, turning it over, seeing her name neatly typed in the center.

"Mrs. Klopher gave it to me, told me to give it to you." She coughed, grabbed a tissue from the drawer, and blew her nose. "I think," she said glumly, "I'm gonna die."

Jennifer smiled. "I think you work too hard," she said as she slipped a folded sheet of pale green paper from the envelope.

"What is it?" Esther asked.

Jennifer read the paragraph typed in the paper's center. "When did she give you this?" she asked.

Esther shrugged. "I don't know. Just after lunch, I guess."

"What?"

The girl nodded. "After lunch. She came in and told me to give it to you."

Jennifer shoved the note into the envelope, and the envelope into her notebook. "Why didn't you give it to me right away?"

"You were working. I didn't want to disturb you. Why, is it important?"

Jennifer groaned silently and rushed outside. She found she was breathing hard, and the sound of a slow wind in the trees was magnified to a roaring. She swallowed, looked to her right toward her dorm, but decided there was no time to hunt for her friends.

She had to go right then; she was almost an hour late.

Beyond the crescent of main buildings, across a lawn marked with small, well-kept flower gardens and isolated evergreen shrubs, were three large houses facing the campus. Each was easily a hundred years old, with large porches both in front and in back, high arched windows, and peaked roofs that bristled with chimneys. The first one Jen passed was white with dark green shutters—the dean's home, deliberately separated from its neighbors by a thick screen of pine trees, a tall hedge, and a low iron gate that opened onto a flagstone walk. Next to it was another house, just as large and painted blue.

The last house on the right was the same, and Jennifer hurried toward it along a narrow stone walk that branched off the circular drive. At the walk's end she turned right, noting that the center house was fully lighted, as if those who lived there were determined to keep the autumn night out by the sheer power of their lamps.

But all the light did was cast shadows.

Holding the books more tightly to her chest, she moved on, ignoring the brown husk of the hedge that rose high above her head and the shadows that blackened the stone. She knew she ought to have taken the time to find Marysue and Monica, but it was too late then.

"Miss Field," the note had said, "if you are as interested in lupines as I am, please come to my rooms at four-thirty today. Do not delay. They don't always travel in packs."

The scrawled signature at the bottom was almost impossible to read, but she would have known it anywhere. It belonged to Pauline Klopher.

It couldn't be a coincidence. The widowed librarian seldom made an effort to get to know any of the students, and certainly could not have mistakenly thought Jennifer was any more fascinated by timber wolves than anyone else.

*They don't always travel in packs.*

The woman knew.

And when Jennifer reached the gap in the hedge that passed for a gate, she did not hesitate. She ran up the steps to the porch and rang the doorbell, looked impatiently at the curtained living room windows, and scowled. It's suppertime, she thought. Someone has to be in. This house, like the one in the center, was divided into several apartments, with a communal kitchen. Boardinghouses for those who had no homes in town or who didn't add to their salaries by living in the dorms to watch over the students.

She stepped closer to the door whose upper half was divided into several faceted, frosted panes and rang the bell again. She couldn't see in; there were curtains there as well.

"C'mon," she whispered. "C'mon, hurry up."

A car engine roared in the parking lot on the other side of the trees near the campus's main entrance.

"C'mon," she muttered, pressing the button a third time and lifting her free hand to knock.

Suddenly the door opened and she stepped back quickly. A tall man stood on the threshold, wearing worn black chinos and a cardigan sweater over an open-necked white shirt and carrying a cup of steaming coffee. He looked too young to be a professor, even with a thick bandit's mustache that seemed ready to swallow his upper lip.

When he saw her, he smiled. "Hello. Miss Field, isn't it?"

"Dr. Overbrook, I'm sorry to bother you, but—"

"No bother at all," he said, stepping aside to let her in. "I was just having some coffee." He looked down at the cup in his hand. "Lousy. This stuff would eat through ten inches of steel."

Her smile was nervous as she sidled into the foyer. She could see no one, and when she looked to the staircase directly ahead she realized she couldn't hear anyone either.

"Right," the man said, setting his cup on a scarred table. "They are all gone. When they remembered it was my turn to cook, they headed for town and a meal that wouldn't kill them." He laughed and reached into a sweater pocket to pull out a pack of cigarettes. "But I don't think you want to know about how bad I am in the kitchen."

"No," she said. Then, flustered, "I mean, yes. I mean—"

He laughed again. "It's all right. I understand. What I don't understand, however, is what you're doing here."

"Mrs. Klopher," she said. "I got a note from her asking me to see her. Here. In her house. Your house, I mean. I mean—"

Borden Overbrook put a hand on her shoulder, his grin wide and his blue eyes filled with mirth. "I'm not going to bite, you know." He led her to a table beside the staircase. On it was a black and chrome intercom system. He lifted the receiver, pressed one of the buttons, and looked at the ceiling as he waited. "This thing is a pain in the neck," he said. "When it works you go deaf, and when it doesn't it takes forever to fix."

Jennifer didn't know what to say. The man's behavior was so radically different from the way he acted in the classroom that she had to keep staring at him to be sure he was, indeed, the man she knew. In class he was stem and refused to accept "I don't know" for an answer, demanding that his students reach the proper conclusions. But this man, the one trying to light a cigarette with one hand while frowning and pressing the button again, didn't look as if he'd be able to yell much louder than a whisper.

"Odd," he said at last, replacing the receiver and cupping a hand over the newel post globe. "I don't remember her going out."

"I didn't see her," Jennifer said. "On the way over, I mean. She wanted to see me at four-thirty. I didn't get the message in time."

Overbrook nodded. "Well, tell you what—I'll pop up and see if she's in, okay?"

"Oh, no," she said. "I don't want to put you to any trouble."

But he was already halfway up the stairs, two steps at a time, and soon vanished around the corner of the landing.

Jennifer backed away to the middle of the foyer and waited, listening to the silence and looking up at the landing.

Dr. Overbrook appeared a moment later, one hand in a pocket, the other gripping the banister.

"Miss Field," he said, "I think you'd better come up here."

# Four

JENNIFER HESITATED AT THE SOLEMN TONE OF HIS voice before starting for the stairs. She paused only long enough to set her books on the table, then hurried up to the landing, made the turn, and paused again at the top. She could see Overbrook's back as he walked away; and aside from his footsteps there was nothing but silence.

Something warned her to leave then, but when she started to turn he called her again, more urgently.

A trap, that same something warned her. It's a trap.

*They know who you are.*

Wishing Lee were there to tell her what to do, she ran down the long, narrow hallway dimly lighted by candle-shaped wall sconces. Overbrook was already near the far end. As she ran to catch up with him, she noted the worn carpet down the floor's center, the closed paneled doors that broke up the walls papered in faded floral patterns.

Overbrook was standing by an open door, staring inside with both hands jammed into the pockets of his sweater.

"What is it?" she asked in a whisper and came to stand beside him.

The room she saw was large and high-ceilinged, the sitting room of an elderly widow. And it looked as if it had been struck by a hurricane.

"Oh, no," she said and followed the man in.

Books were strewn all over the fringed carpet, papers and pages scattered on the chairs and love seat. A portable television set on a tripod stand had been pulled away from the wall, a shortwave radio lay on its face in one corner. A door on the right was open to a bedroom, and Overbrook motioned her to stay where she was while he went in. But from where she stood it looked the same—ransacked.

"It's this house," he said when he returned. "It's so big I didn't hear a thing. The walls have to be nine feet thick, they're so old." He glanced around again, shaking his head. "She's not there. Are you sure she wanted to meet you here, not at the library or the Union?"

Jennifer could do nothing but nod. Her throat had gone dry. He said something about checking the other apartment on the floor, but she didn't move. She could only stare and feel a cold needle draw down her spine.

Would this have happened to her own room the other night if she hadn't interrupted the intruder?

Then she blinked and realized she was alone. A gasp, and she whirled to get out, stopped short of the threshold when she saw a balled-up sheet of pale green paper on the floor, crammed against the wall by the open door. Without thinking, she picked it up, smoothed it out, and saw a list written in pencil down one side. Opposite most of the items were tiny checkmarks; two of them had none.

"This is most irregular, Borden," a thin voice said in the hallway, and Jennifer shoved the paper into her waistband just as Overbrook returned, followed by a small man in shirtsleeves and suspenders, his head more scalp than hair, his eyes squinting behind a pair of wire-rimmed glasses.

When he saw her he scowled. "Young lady, you do not belong here."

"Take it easy, Martin," Overbrook said. "I asked her up when I saw this." He stepped aside, and the elderly man peered into the room.

"Oh, my goodness," he said, mouth wide in shock. "What happened?"

"Well, Martin, it looks like a burglary, doesn't *it*? I don't suppose you heard anything either."

"I was napping," the man said stiffly. "I'm under doctor's orders, as you well know. If I had heard, I certainly wouldn't have gone back to sleep."

Overbrook shrugged. "Well, I guess I'll have to get in touch with the police." He smiled at Jennifer and waved her out to the hall.

Martin Ellis hurried after them, his hands flapping nervously at his sides. "Police! Really, Borden, I don't think the dean would appreciate the police, not here. It wouldn't—"

"I know he wouldn't appreciate it," Overbrook said with a wink at Jennifer. "But this is a police matter, and I'm sure Dean Dramon will have no complaints."

"I'm not so sure," the older man muttered, but said nothing more when Borden walked down the stairs and picked up the phone to call the Staines police.

As he spoke, giving all the particulars he could, Jennifer watched Dr. Ellis come down the stairs, wring his hands for a moment, then square his shoulders and march out the front door. It slammed behind him just as Overbrook finished, and the man frowned.

"The old fool," he said without heat. "Y'know, Miss Field, I think he'd be much happier living in the nineteenth century." The frown was replaced by a smile, and he nodded toward a narrow doorway. "I guess we're stuck here until the police come. Would you like something to drink?"

"Sir?"

"Soda," he said, laughing. "Or coffee. Tea? Whatever it is you kids drink these days."

She followed him meekly into a large, bright, thoroughly modern kitchen decorated in brown, copper, and touches of subdued yellow. After hesitating, she sat at a round table near the back door. She was shaking and couldn't stop; she was afraid for Mrs. Klopher and understood that whatever had happened upstairs had something to do with the message in the envelope.

She prayed for Lee to come strolling in unannounced.

She wished Marysue or Monica would come after her.

She watched as Overbrook fussed at the stove, humming to himself, then brought two steaming cups over to the table. After checking to be sure he hadn't forgotten anything, he turned his chair around, with the back against the table, and straddled the seat.

"Hot chocolate," he said. "I know it's old-fashioned, but it really does wonders for the nerves." Then his voice softened. "Are you all right, Miss Field?"

After a moment, she nodded and sipped gratefully at the hot liquid.

A large round clock hummed over the refrigerator.

Overbrook folded his hands around his cup and looked at her until she finally met his eyes. "I don't suppose you'd like to tell me what your meeting was about."

She shook her head. "I don't know," she said and cleared her throat when it sounded as if her voice would crack. "I really don't, honestly. I got this message—late, like I said—and I came right over."

"I see." His left hand slowly brushed over his mustache. "Odd, isn't it."

She nodded, sipped her drink again, and nearly dropped her cup when the door swung open with a slam against the wall and Dr. Ellis burst in. He stopped when he saw them at the table, and he lifted a hand as if to shoo them away.

"Now really, Overbrook, this is most irregular indeed. First that student is upstairs where she has no business, and now she's in the privacy of our kitchen. I really must protest."

Borden didn't turn, but he did wink again. "The young lady, Martin, has had quite a shock, in case you'd forgotten. She came here for a meeting with Pauline and finds herself now in the middle of a police investigation. I don't think you'd begrudge her a little hot chocolate, would you?"

Ellis opened his mouth to protest, but Jennifer was on her feet and pointing to a free chair. "Please," she said. "Have a seat for a minute. I'll get you some chocolate. You look awfully cold."

Before he could respond, she took a cup and saucer from the cupboard. She knew that what she was about to do would be dangerous, but the idea had come to her just as Dr. Ellis had entered the room. She could be caught, or she could suffer embarrassment, and the latter was definitely better than the former.

If her idea worked.

Quickly she mixed powder and warm milk, put the spoon on the saucer, and took a deep breath.

I can't, she told herself.

You have to.

Another deep breath, and she realized the two men were watching her strangely.

Well, Field, she told herself, if you're going to do it, don't wait for an invitation.

She carried the drink over, set it down with a big smile in front of Dr. Ellis, and headed back to her own seat, passing behind Overbrook on the way. Suddenly she gave a short cry and fell heavily against him, twisting so that her elbows landed firmly against his sides. He grunted, and his arm swung out to catch her before she hit the floor.

"Oh, I'm sorry," she said, backing away quickly and pushing her hair from her eyes. "I'm really sorry. My legs . . . they just gave out. I'm sorry. Really."

"Hey, it's all right," the man said, a puzzled expression on his face when she grinned at him. "Just sit down before you decide to kick the chair out from under me."

Ellis merely stared at them, obviously disapproving.

"Really, I'm sorry," Jennifer whispered again as she took her seat, clasping her hands tightly in her lap when she realized they were trembling too much for her to pick the cup up.

Her smile was strained.

She found it hard to take a breath.

She called herself an idiot, yet felt a great relief that she had put the plan to use for the first time and had been able to eliminate Borden Overbrook from suspicion.

"Miss Field," Dr. Ellis began, but he stopped when the doorbell rang.

"The police," Overbrook said.

Immediately both men got to their feet and left the room.

As soon as they were gone, she pulled the ball of paper from her waistband and spread it carefully on the table, frowning as she tried to interpret Mrs. Klopher's hasty scrawl. But when she finally held the paper close to her eyes, she was able to read most of it.

And when she was done she was no wiser than before.

1. Gymnasium
2. North field
3. W.E.
4. Union basement
5. W. Marsh
6. Staines park (south?)
7. B. Hill
8. Pool
9. Staines (too big, impossible)
10. Old science building (debris, check cellar)

The checkmarks she had noted before were beside every item except "Union basement" and "W.E." The initials meant nothing to her, but she knew that the other shortened names were Winter's Marsh, a swampy ten acres in the forest on the school's northern boundary, and Ballad Hill, which rose above the highway directly across from the main gates.

"W.E.," she whispered, as if saying the letters aloud would bring recognition. "W.E."

Then she shrugged. Right then the most important thing was to find Mrs. Klopher. The purpose of the list would come in time.

And again she shoved the paper into her waistband when Dr. Overbrook poked his head in and told her that the police wanted to have a word with her.

Nervously she wiped her palms on her jeans, pulled her sweater closed over her chest, and walked into the hallway. Ten minutes later she was back in the kitchen, blinking at the abruptness of it all, and pleased that the investigators had believed her when she said she hadn't a clue about what had happened.

She listened to them talking in the hallway, listened as they marched up and down the stairs, and managed a brief smile each time Overbrook looked in to see how she was doing. The detective in charge had asked her not to leave in case other questions arose, and by the end of the first hour she was ready to scream.

Voices in the hall, on the stairs, and outside where flashlights darted across the ground.

She sat, she stood, she wished they would let her go back to her room and was readying her courage to ask them just that when, suddenly, they were gone.

One minute they were bustling all over, and the next the house was silent.

She rose from the table and bit down on her lower lip, started for the door, and stopped with a small cry when it swung open and Dr. Overbrook came in, her books in his hands.

"All clear," he said, handing them over.

"Did they . . . find anything?"

"Not a thing," he said, scratching the side of his neck. "Not a thing. But," he added as she started to go around him, "would you mind telling me something?"

She looked at him and frowned. "What?"

"Would you mind telling me what you took from her room?"

# Five

THE CLOCK HUMMED.

The refrigerator snapped on with a muffled rattling.

The impulse to deny she had taken anything died as soon as she saw the look on his face. He was not menacing or threatening, but his expression and the tilt of his head told her he had seen her pick up the paper, had known about it all along—though, for reasons of his own, he hadn't said a word.

Her next thought was to insist that it was nothing, that it didn't mean a thing, but again she knew that wouldn't do. She shrugged, sighed, and showed him what she'd found.

The refrigerator snapped off, and the silence was too loud.

"Interesting," he said when he had finished reading. "What is it?"

"I don't know."

He looked doubtful.

"Really," she said earnestly. "I really don't. It was behind the door in the corner. I just . . . picked it up."

"I see. Miss Field," he said at last, in a voice too close to the one he used in the classroom, "I think, before anything else happens, you'd better tell me what's going on."

"What? I don't know what you're talking about."

41

For the first time that night he was angry, his eyes narrowing and his lips thinning to a bloodless line. "Jennifer, listen to me—not all teachers are like Dr. Ellis. Some of us have not yet fallen screaming into old age. Some of us, believe it or not, are actually quite aware of what's going on in the outside world, even when we're in a small, out-of-the-way place like Thaler. And ever since I arrived here, I've seen more curiosities than I've ever seen in my life."

"Curiosities?" she asked quietly.

"I think you know what I'm talking about, Jennifer, and I would appreciate it if you wouldn't treat me as if I were a fool. I may have been one for accepting this post, but that doesn't mean I am one every waking moment of my life."

Suddenly he smiled.

"Look," he said, gripping the edge of the table, "there's a mystery here involving Mrs. Klopher and, like it or not, we both seem to be involved. She's gone, her apartment's torn apart, and no one has the slightest idea what's happened. Except, perhaps, you."

"But I don't," she insisted. "I really don't."

"But you do know more than the rest of us. And I think, for her sake, you ought to tell someone."

Jennifer looked from side to side helplessly. She knew they had planned to talk with Overbrook eventually, but now that the moment had been dumped in her lap, she wasn't sure how to proceed.

"Miss Field?"

He passed the test, she reminded herself.

But he would think she was crazy; he would think they were all crazy.

"Jennifer," he said quietly. "I really do want to help."

"I don't know," she answered.

He waited.

"Dr. Overbrook, I . . ." She stood with her books held to her chest, ready to bolt, afraid.

If *they* found out . . .

If *they* knew what she was doing . . .

But he had passed the test!

Borden walked to the stove, heated up another pan of milk, and made another two cups of hot chocolate. All without a word, without a single glance in her direction. Then he sat at the table and spread the paper in front of him, frowning as he read each item aloud, one hand cupped at the back of his head.

"Looks to me," he said, "as if she was hunting for something, and I don't think it was a pair of earrings, do you?"

She couldn't speak; she only shook her head.

"Right. In that case, these could be places she's already checked, the ones that are marked off." His hand came around to his mustache and stroked it thoughtfully. "Here," he said, still without looking up, "she says Staines is too big. For what? To search thoroughly? And what's this about an old science building and some debris? I don't remember seeing one around here. What the hell is 'W.E.'? What's 'B. Hill'?"

"Ballad Hill," she said, barely loudly enough for him to hear. "It's the hill across the road."

"Ah."

And still he didn't look up.

"Ah."

Then, so slowly she barely knew she was moving, she found herself walking toward the table, clutching her books hard to her chest, so hard the edges dug into her skin and made her wince.

"What in heaven's name," he said, "is so fascinating about the basement of the Student Union? Nothing but spiders."

She didn't know what it was—the tone of his voice, the actual words—but she ran the rest of the way over and dropped her books on the table. He looked up, startled, and nodded once as she sat down opposite him.

"Wolves," she said, pulling the envelope out of her notebook.

"Wolves?" he repeated. "What about them?"

She let him read Mrs. Klopher's message, her gaze on his face, looking for a reaction that would tell her she'd just made the worst mistake of her life.

When he finished he placed it beside the list and stared at her.

"Wolves," he said again. "I don't get it."

There was a bubble in Jennifer's chest, one that expanded slowly and painfully as she struggled between caution and the desire to let someone else know, to shift part of the nightmare's burden off her shoulders. She wanted to cry, and she wanted to scream, and the bubble continued to grow until suddenly she sat back, straight, her palms flat on the table before her.

Borden's expression changed when he saw her distress, and he reached out to cover her hands with his—briefly, just long enough to let her know he was willing to listen.

He passed the test, she thought.

The bubble burst.

And she told him.

Everything.

\* \* \*

It was almost nine o'clock by the time she was finished, and she marveled that they hadn't been interrupted in all that time. She had heard no doors opening or closing, no footsteps in the hall or foyer, and she had to look at the clock twice to be sure she wasn't mistaken.

Overbrook said nothing.

He had shifted several times during the telling, but he had not asked a single question, made a single comment, hadn't even made a single sound to distract her. He only watched and listened, and once in a while nodded when she stumbled through an explanation that, to her ears, sounded like a lunatic's ravings.

And when it was over, she slumped in her chair, exhausted and fearful, waiting for his response.

And still he said nothing.

A glance at the clock, a look at the watch on his wrist, and he took out a cigarette, lit it, and stared at the gray smoke curling toward the ceiling.

"What," he said then, "would you do if I told you I was one of them?"

She gaped. Her heart turned to lead and her breath to fire, and tears sprang to her eyes as she pushed back her chair.

"No," he said hastily, when he saw her ready to run. "No, I'm not. You've already proven that, I think. But what would you have done if I were?"

It came out before she could stop it: "Killed you. Or tried to." Her voice sounded like an old woman's, and she cleared her throat twice before speaking again. "Before you killed me. Which you would have."

He nodded thoughtfully, looked at the two papers, and flicked an ash on the floor. When he saw her look, he grinned. "It drives Dr. Ellis crazy."

The silly remark brought a giggle to her lips, and then a full laugh that spilled her tears and dispelled her fears. She wanted to leap up and hug the man in gratitude. But she stopped herself and calmed down as quickly as she could.

"You . . . you believe me?" she asked.

"You believe it," he answered.

"Oh."

"And your friends do. And," he said, pointing the cigarette at the papers, "so, apparently, did Pauline. As you say—there's no reason why she would think you were interested in real wolves, the kind that howl at the full moon. So she must have found out all or some of what you already knew and wanted to help you. Or to give you information she knew you didn't have."

Jennifer agreed quickly. "Yes, but how did she know we knew, and why didn't she tell the authorities? I mean, telling us wouldn't do any good."

"Maybe she couldn't," he said. "Maybe she never had a chance or, like you, didn't have the proof."

"But she's a grown-up," she protested. "Someone would have believed her, right?"

Borden smiled sadly. "Alas, you overestimate the power of growing up, Jennifer. Institutions all over the world are filled with so-called adults who have tried to warn the world of things only they knew.

"Don't misunderstand me, Jennifer. I'm not saying you and Pauline are crazy. Obviously someone was willing to take the chance of discovery to search Pauline's room for whatever she had found."

"Do you think they've killed her?"

"I haven't the slightest idea. But the police don't; they think she's probably just out for the evening, and when she comes back she'll find her place a mess and call them. Meanwhile, they'll keep an eye out for her."

"But—"

"As I said, with no sign of what they call foul play, what else can they do? So far it's only breaking and entering, and none of us even knows if anything's been taken."

Except, she thought, Mrs. Klopher.

Overbrook looked up at the clock. "It's getting late. The rest of the house should be returning soon, and I don't think your reputation will be done any good if they see you here, talking with a crusty old bachelor, alone."

"You're not so old," she said and clamped a hand to her mouth when he laughed. "I mean—"

"No," he told her. "Please, don't explain. Compliments like that don't come along every day. Let me have the memory, if nothing else."

She smiled and ducked her head when she felt herself beginning to blush. This was silly. He was a grown man, and she was acting like some stupid kid.

Then he stood, folded the two papers, and placed them inside her notebook. "If I take them," he explained as he handed it all over, "you'll think I'll destroy them and then deny they ever existed. I want you and your friends to trust me, Jennifer. We can't do anything if you don't."

"Does that mean you'll help us?"

"It means that, under the circumstances, I don't have much choice."

She wanted to hug him, hugged her books instead, and followed him out of the kitchen into the foyer. The house was silent around them, and she couldn't wait to tell Lee and the others that she'd solved their first problem.

He reached for the doorknob and lifted an eyebrow. "Needless to say, Jennifer—not a word."

"No, honest."

"And if you can, meet me, with your friends, after my last class tomorrow. About three. In . . . let's say, in my lab."

She nodded, backed away as he pulled the door open, and shivered at the ghost of cold air that crept into the house.

"Be careful," he cautioned as she stepped onto the porch.

"Indeed," a voice said beside her. "One never knows about the dark, Miss Field. Do indeed be careful."

She whirled, stumbled, and couldn't find her voice when Peter Dramon stepped out of the shadows and took hold of her arm.

# Six

JENNIFER DID HER BEST NOT TO RUN ALL THE WAY back to the dorm.

Dean Dramon had smiled at her there in the shadows of the porch, as if the grip on her arm was to prevent her from stumbling. Then, with a look to the night sky, he had cautioned her again about roaming around in the dark and let her go. She had frozen for several seconds. She had to swallow to get her heart back in its place. Then she hurried down the steps and, at the head of the walk, turned to see him standing in the doorway. The light from the foyer had turned him into a black silhouette, but she knew he was watching her. Carefully. Steadily. That horrid faint smile still on his lips.

When she turned away, she heard the front door close, and the light from the house disappeared, leaving her nothing but the moon.

Her first chilling thought was that the dean had finally marked her after all this time. Because of her presence in the faculty boardinghouse, she was no longer regarded as just a nuisance and had been marked for elimination. As others had been once they had discovered the truth. Her second thought was that now the professor was marked as well, and it was all her fault.

She glanced back over her shoulder.

Her heels were loud on the walk; her breath came in puffs of short-lived fog.

A patrol car was parked down near the campus entrance; another was in front of the administration building, empty, its radio spitting bursts of static into the cold night air. She stared at it for a moment before moving on, remembering the policeman they had once trusted who had turned out to be an alien. She assumed he was the only one on the force. Their presence on campus was a comfort that night.

By the time she reached the dorm she had dismissed the idea that Overbrook was in trouble. The dean couldn't know what she had told the man, and Overbrook didn't seem the type to let everyone in on what he was thinking until he was good and ready.

Some of the girls were standing on the porch in scarves and coats, speculating on the reasons for the police being there. When they asked if she knew anything, Jennifer denied it with a shrug and ran upstairs, dumped her books in her room, and ran up the hall to pound on Marysue's door. There was no answer, and the door was locked; she tried Monica's as well and received the same response.

Where are they? she thought, swinging between panic and elation; she had tremendous news, and there was no one to tell.

Then she snapped her fingers, ran downstairs to the wall of telephones, and snatched one from its cradle. She had dialed Lee's number before she saw the hand-printed "Out of Order" sign taped to the wall. She tried each of the others, glared at them, and slammed them down in frustration. A line must be down, she thought.

She searched the ground floor. It was empty—no one in the study room, no one in the common room. They were all outside.

With a groan of frustration, she returned upstairs and tried several other girls, but no one had seen Beauford since dinner, and no one had seen Holt at all.

"Great," she muttered to herself. "Just great."

Back at her own desk, she looked blindly out the window toward the forested hills behind the school. The stars were brilliant, the moon almost bright enough to let her pick out individual trees, and she sat for nearly an hour, letting her mind drift, waiting for someone to get back, until with a start she realized she was falling asleep.

She gave a yawn and prepared for bed, tried one more time to locate either of the other girls, then crawled wearily under the blankets.

Tomorrow, she thought. Tomorrow will be plenty of time to tell them the news.

The next morning she woke up later than usual and rushed through her dressing. But neither Monica nor Marysue was in her room or in the dining hall. Panic returned until she found someone who had seen Beauford only a few minutes before, yet searching for her almost made Jennifer late for her first class.

She didn't hear a word in class and was twice scolded for her inattention.

She tried the other phones in other buildings to call Lee, but most were out of order as well, and the few that worked had students waiting in line to use them.

By the time her morning classes were over, she felt so restless she was ready to scream. She was debating whether to skip lunch when a sudden thought sent her up the stairs to the library.

Esther was behind the desk.

"Hi," the chubby girl said brightly. "Can you believe this? I'm actually in charge during the hours I work!"

"But what about—"

Esther shrugged. "Beats me. I heard she was in Staines, talking to the cops. Boy, I'd hate to be the guy who has to tell her they can't find the jerk who robbed her. She'll absolutely kill him. I mean, she'll string the poor sucker up."

Jennifer grinned and left, taking the stairs slowly. She was beginning to feel as if her friends were avoiding her, then scolded herself for being foolish. She ran back to write a note to each of them, telling them where she'd be at three, demanding they drop everything and be there, without fail. She slipped the papers under their doors, at the last minute decided to take the list she'd found in Mrs. Klopher's room, and headed for her last class of the day—math—in the science building.

On the dot of three the bell finally rang to signal the end of class. She grabbed her books off the desk, zipped out of the classroom before any of the others, and took the staircase down into the basement.

Here, in a warren of rooms wider than the building above it, were most of the laboratories—for physics, chemistry, and biology. Overbrook's, at the far end, was little more than a classroom with display cases, chairs, tables, and a slate-topped table and sink at the front from which he demonstrated ecology chains.

At the first session he had laughed and called it Overbrook's Dungeon, and more than one student wondered why a supposedly important man had been stuck off in a corner. The puzzle fed a great number of rumors, not the least of which was that he was hiding out from a scandal so terrible it had been deliberately kept out of the papers.

She entered without knocking and smiled when she saw the teacher standing in front of a ceiling-high display case in which were kept bell jars containing various examples of plants and insects found in Thaler's immediate area. The plants were dead, examples, the teacher had told his classes, of what happened when man tried to make the earth into his own image of paradise. Also examples of dying without air.

He turned when he heard her, nodded without returning her smile, and motioned her over.

"Last night after you left," he said without greeting her, "I had a talk with the dean. Mr. Ellis had obviously gone to get him."

His expression was somber, with none of that mocking tone in his voice. Overbrook fingered his mustache. "He warned me about you."

"Warned you?"

"That wherever you go, trouble seems to tag along."

She knew suddenly that the dean was probably preparing the grounds for her expulsion—after all, what better way to get her out of his hair than to send her back home? Who would believe in aliens there? Who could she turn to when all the proof, if there was proof at all, was here on campus?

Yet in one sense she was relieved because it meant that her fears of being killed were groundless. It would be better for them simply to ship her away to a place where she'd be harmless. Another student death would call too much attention to the school.

"It was also obvious," he said with a shrug, "that it was a warning to me as well."

Before she could ask what he was talking about, the door burst open and Lee rushed in. Immediately she ran across the room and into his arms, startling him into dropping a long paper tube he was holding. Then, just as quickly, she realized where she was and what she was doing, stepped back, and glared at him. "Why haven't you called me?" she demanded. "Do you have any idea how much I've wanted to talk to you? Do you know what's—"

"Hey," he said as he bent over to retrieve the tube, "lighten up, huh? I'm not a mind reader."

"What?" She was so relieved, and so furious, she was nearly in tears. "How can I, Lee, when—"

"Jennifer, Lee was just on an errand for me. There's no need to snap his head off."

She saw again the paper in Lee's hand. "What's that?" she asked.

"A map."

She frowned.

He walked to the table and unrolled the tube, pinning down the corners with books. Overbrook joined them, and when she looked down she saw it was a map of the valley and the surrounding hills.

"I was just in the library," Lee muttered. "Dr. Overbrook wanted this map. And, boy, is that Esther nosy. You'd think I was trying to break into Fort Knox or something. I had to sign forty-two forms just to take the stupid thing out."

She gave him an apologetic smile just as Marysue came in, a large book in her arms. She puffed to the table and dumped it with a bang. "Nobody," she said, "should have to read anything this big. It would be like going to prison. Hey, Jenny."

"The library, right?" she said.

"Well, where else, child? Do you think I keep something like this under my bed?"

In confusion Jennifer turned to Overbrook, who only looked at her and asked, "Do you have the list?"

Silently she took it from her notebook while the man told the others only what had happened to Mrs. Klopher's rooms at the boardinghouse the night before, leaving out specifics. Then he let them all read the items the librarian had scribbled down. And no one, not even Lee, knew what W.E. stood for.

And only Jennifer saw the puzzled, suspicious look on Lee's face.

"Therefore," Overbrook said to her, smiling at last, "the map. I'm assuming it's a place since everything else on the list is. And if it's a place, and local, it's got to be here."

They spent half an hour poring over the large map section by section, and they found nothing.

"It's got to be," Overbrook kept saying as he checked for the third and fourth times. "It's got to be."

"Maybe it does," Lee said at last, "but I'd like to know why you're so interested."

Jennifer realized that Overbrook had told the others nothing, had only asked them to run errands they had obviously assumed were for class. Then, with a nod from the instructor, she explained that she had told Overbrook everything they had learned about the aliens after she had checked to be sure he wasn't one.

But Lee was still not fully convinced. "You believed her awfully quick," he said. "I mean, you haven't even seen one of these things, and you still believed her."

Borden leaned against the table. He stared down at the map, then looked up at them without raising his head.

"You're right, Mr. Fawkes," he said finally. "As I told Miss Field last night, I'm willing to believe only that there's something very odd going on around here, and that I'm willing to keep a perfectly open mind about everything until

I know more. And I *am* willing because Pauline Klopher is a friend, and I want to know what happened to her."

Lee was still doubtful, but he relented when Jennifer put a hand on his arm. "We need him," she said quietly. "We all agreed we need him."

At that moment, the door crashed open.

Jennifer spun around with a cry at her lips, her eyes wide, when she saw Conrad standing on the threshold.

"Mrs. Klopher," the boy gasped. "Come, quickly."

# Seven

CONRAD GAVE THEM NO TIME FOR QUESTIONS, NOR did he wait to explain. He ran back out.

After grabbing their coats they followed him in confusion, up the stairs and across the lawn to his car parked on the drive, its right front wheel up over the curb. The engine was still running.

"Zucco," Marysue said.

"Later!" he told her.

"But—"

"Just get in, okay? Just get in!"

The automobile, which ran only half the time, was at least eight years old, red, rusted through on the fenders, and small, barely large enough for Conrad, much less all of them. As soon as he saw it, Overbrook pulled the boy to one side, asked where they were going, nodded several times, and ran for the faculty parking lot. Conrad jumped in behind the steering wheel and raced off, tires squealing and causing more than a few heads to turn in his direction.

Jennifer was in the backseat with Lee, holding his hand tightly, while Marysue, in front, gripped the dashboard with both hands.

Suddenly Jennifer looked worried. "Monica," she said. "We forgot Monica."

"Too late," Lee told her. "We can't stop now. We'll have to fill her in later."

"But I haven't seen her all day!" she protested. "She doesn't know anything about what's going on, and this was all her idea. Marysue?"

Beauford shrugged without moving her hands from the dash. "Don't look at me. The last time I saw her was last night. She said she was going swimming."

At the back of the gymnasium was a new addition— an Olympic-sized heated swimming pool; its roof was a dome of translucent green glass. It was open all day and well beyond classroom hours for those who wanted the exercise or needed the relaxation.

No wonder I couldn't find her, Jennifer thought.

"Well, are you gonna talk or what?" Beauford said to Conrad when they'd swung out of the gates onto the highway, turning away from the valley and Staines. "What's this about Mrs. Klopher?"

Conrad, his face pale and his hands white-knuckled on the steering wheel, swallowed heavily as he maneuvered the tiny vehicle around a sharp right-hand bend in the road. "I was getting ready for class this afternoon," he said, "when I got this call. I didn't recognize the voice at first, but . . . it was her. It was Mrs. Klopher."

"What?" Jennifer and Lee asked.

"I couldn't believe it either," he said with a quick shake of his head. "I thought she was after some book or something I hadn't brought back on time. But she sounded . . . I don't know. She sounded scared. And really mad too. She said she had to meet us. She told me where to go, and we were cut off."

Oh no, Jennifer thought.

"She said you'd know what she was talking about, Jen. I hope so, but I sure don't."

"Yes," she said. "It's—"

"Wait a minute," Lee said, trying to keep from falling over into her lap when the car swerved through another curve. He pulled up his denim jacket sleeve. "Wait a minute, that must have been almost two hours ago."

"Yeah, I know," Conrad said, tight-lipped. "On the way out I got stopped for speeding."

Marysue patted his shoulder. "The Lone Ranger never had that kind of trouble. You should stick to bicycles, like Lee."

"It was Rumbel, Lee."

Lee groaned, saw Jennifer's questioning gaze, and shrugged his disgust. "You ever see those dumb movies where the southern cop is a fat-headed jerk that hates anyone under thirty? Well, this guy's in New England, but he's the same. He's the mayor's cousin or something, which is why they haven't fired him, I think."

"Is he that bad?" Marysue asked.

He snorted in disgust. "Are you kidding? I mean, all he has to do is catch you jaywalking, and he practically takes your whole life history like you were a mass murderer and gives you the third degree just because he likes it."

They looked at each other then, and she knew he was thinking the same thing—that another cop, Larry Ives, who'd known Lee for quite a while, had turned out to be one of the creatures. He was gone now, but the memory remained.

Was it a coincidence then, that just as Conrad was racing for help he was stopped and held so long?

"I don't know," Conrad said as if he'd read their minds. "I don't know."

Jennifer checked the rear window—Overbrook's car was nowhere in sight. Lee saw her and squeezed her hand, to tell her the instructor would be along and to let her know he was there too.

The road straightened, curved again, and continued its gentle downward progress, sweeping in stages around the contours of Ballad Hill. No traffic passed them in the opposite direction, and the forest there came straight to the shoulder, leaving little room for maneuvering should a car leave the blacktop.

Then Marysue yelped when the car bounced over a fallen rock, and yelped again when Conrad suddenly put his foot on the brakes and the rear end fishtailed until he brought the car back under control.

"Sorry. Almost missed it," he said sheepishly and nodded toward a small side road virtually hidden by trees and shrubs. "She's in there."

The narrow, nameless road they followed next had never been paved, and decades of neglect had broken it into stretches of rutted dirt mixed with winter-tossed rocks entwined with weeds. Low-hanging branches scraped loudly along the roof and scratched at the windows, bushes dug at the undercarriage, making Conrad wince as he moved along as fast as he could.

The autumn foliage was still on most of the trees they passed, and the late-afternoon light was dim and tinted with gold.

"I remember this," Lee said suddenly. "My dad used to come here, I think."

"Yeah," said Conrad, his shoulders hunched as if taking the blows from the trees himself. "I thought you would. I wonder how she knew about it, though."

"Beats me."

"Well," Marysue said when neither of them seemed inclined to elaborate. "Are you going to let us in on the secret, or is it a surprise?"

Conrad grinned.

Lee looked at Jennifer, who was staring out the back window, wondering what had happened to Borden Overbrook.

"There's a small lake back here," Conrad finally explained. "It's too little for real development stuff, like for summer houses and things, but it's large enough for fishermen to come out on weekends and sit around and drink. They haven't done that for a while, though. A few years ago the lake died."

"What?" Marysue stared at him. "It died?"

"You haven't been listening in class, Miss Beauford," he answered in perfect imitation of Overbrook's stern reprimand. "The spring that fed it dried up for some reason, so there's no way for the water to get out except by evaporation. Except for rain, there was no way to replace it with fresh water. Algae started growing on the surface and the oxygen below was gone before you knew it. The fish died. The weeds took over. The lake died. And that," he said with a grin, "is called ecology. Miss Beauford."

She punched his arm, not lightly, then cringed as the car passed between two monstrous boulders. "And Mrs. Klopher's out here?"

"That's what she said." Then he glanced into the rearview mirror. "What I want to know is, why'd she call me? And where did she call from?"

Jennifer, distracted from her futile search for Overbrook, quickly explained what had happened the night before and did her best to remember all the items on the librarian's list. Conrad whistled softly and slowed the car even more as they approached a clearing.

" 'Curiouser and curiouser,' " he said quietly. Then he looked at Marysue with another grin. "*Alice in Wonderland*. That's literature."

Marysue stuck her tongue out at him and drew her jacket more tightly over her chest.

"Rumbel," Lee said. He looked at Jennifer. "Was he one of the cops that you saw last night? Big guy. Beer gut, fat nose, wears his hair like a marine?"

She shook her heard. "There was a detective, I guess, and a couple of patrolmen. But I didn't see anybody like that."

"Okay," he said and sat back, arms crossed over his chest as his eyes narrowed in thought.

When it was obvious he wasn't going to say any more, she leaned forward to peer through the windshield and saw the lake. Conrad was right—it was small, not much larger than a pond.

"Ugh," Marysue muttered.

It was little more than a hundred yards across, much of its surface coated with the green algae that had finally killed it. Willows and birch overhung its shoreline on the far side, but on the near side the trees were less dense, the grass low and covered with fallen leaves.

Conrad parked the car just short of breaking into the open, and they sat for a long moment, waiting for someone to greet them or chase them off.

A crow squawked overhead.

They got out slowly and walked cautiously into the open. There was no sense in trying to sneak up—the leaves, the twigs, the storm-dropped branches would announce their arrival long before they were spotted, if the noise of the car's engine hadn't done so already.

Had it been another time, Jennifer knew she would have savored the beauty of the secluded spot. The explosion of colors in the foliage against the stark blue of the late-afternoon sky were almost picture-postcard perfect. There was even a pair of ducks swimming lazily on the far side of the lake, now dipping their heads below the surface to feed, now calling softly to each other.

They stood close together, shivering in the chilled air and staring toward the walls of a pair of roughly built single-room log cabins, one on either side of the road that vanished long before it reached the water. Shelter for the fishermen, Conrad explained in a whisper, and she wondered how much protection they could have provided since the roof of one had collapsed, and the other roof was pocked with gaping holes.

There was no sign of anyone.

And when the noise of their arrival faded into the woods, the silence was complete.

"Well?" Lee said finally.

Jennifer started for the lefthand cabin, the one with some of its roof still attached. There were no windows on the side nearest them, and around the front there were only three steps made of cinder blocks leading to the closed front door. A glance up, and Jennifer saw a tottering chimney; a glance to her right, and she saw the clear remains of a campfire—a circle of stones and a shallow pit in which charred wood still lay.

Lee saw it as well and motioned Conrad and Marysue to go to the back of the cabin, circle around, and meet them at the front door. Beauford was reluctant, but Conrad grabbed her hand and pulled her away.

Jennifer rubbed her palms together to bring them some warmth.

The ducks left the water in a flurry of wings, and Jennifer jumped. To the left of the door was a narrow window, its upper pane intact, a gap in the lower one stuffed with a rag whose ends fluttered in the breeze. She stared at it hard, but could see no one or nothing inside.

When she looked at Lee, he shrugged.

When the others came around the far corner and shook their heads, she took a deep breath and walked up to the door.

This is dumb, she thought as she reached for the latch; it could be a trap, they could have guns, we could disappear and no one would ever find us.

This is dumb, she thought again and shoved the door open.

# Eight

"Jenny, wait a minute," Lee said anxiously. "Hang on, will you?"

But it was too late. She was already up the steps, the door swinging back on its hinges and slamming against the wall.

The cabin was empty.

As they stepped gingerly over the threshold, they could see straight ahead a wide-mouthed fieldstone fireplace in which three large logs had been laid over a pile of kindling. A box of matches was on its side between the feet of one of a pair of black andirons. A small metal kettle lay beside the logs.

To the right was the room's only window, its upper pane dimmed with layers of dust through which they could barely see the other cabin; in a corner was a pile of rags, faded and stiff.

Jennifer shivered. It was, she thought, like walking into an open refrigerator.

Spider webs, heavy with prey wrapped in filmy white, clogged the high corners and hung between the open, rough beams; pillars of pale, dust-filled light dropped from the half-dozen holes in the peaked roof, and once their eyes adjusted they could see, to one side of the raised stone hearth, a tin plate and cup, both dented and obviously long unused.

"Brother," Lee whispered.

"Gross," Marysue said.

The dust and tracked-in dirt on the uneven floor was thick, so they could tell that someone had been in there recently—there were faint footprints by the window and in the corners, and several smudged areas around the fireplace.

They jumped when a squirrel chattered angrily at them through one of the holes above them, and they looked sheepishly at one another when the animal bounded away, its claws loud and its voice comical now because it sounded as if it were muttering to itself.

Marysue held Conrad's arm tightly as they crossed to check the window. She moved as if she were trying not to touch a thing, including the floor, and he was scowling, frequently looking back at the open door, sagging slightly on its rusted hinges. Lee caught the look and stayed at the threshold, glancing outside as much as he scanned the cabin itself.

No one said a word.

No one had to.

It took less than five minutes to convince themselves there was no possible way anyone could hide in there; there were no traps in the floor, no hidden closets, no secret rooms behind the fireplace or under the hearth. And they shared a common thought: if Pauline Klopher had been using this for sanctuary, there was no sign she was anywhere near it now.

Marysue was the first to return outside, and she took a deep breath, bent over, and took another. "It's like an attic in there," she said when the others joined her. "It smells like it's a hundred years old."

Conrad touched Lee's arm and gave a nod to the girls to stay where they were. He and Lee walked toward the second cabin, slightly apart, and not slowing when Lee reached down to pick up a stout length of fallen branch.

"She's got to be around here someplace," Jennifer whispered. "She just has to."

Marysue shook her head slowly. "Maybe . . . maybe they found out where she was."

Jennifer didn't want to consider the possibility and knew she had to—just as she had to wonder if, in fact, the call had only been a trick to get them out there alone. They had been so anxious to find the librarian that none of them had bothered to consider that fact.

But before she could say anything, a guttural roaring exploded the woods' silence, and when they whirled around they saw a motorcycle bouncing along the road toward them.

Instantly the two boys ducked into the second cabin, while Jennifer grabbed Marysue's hand and pulled her around the side of the first one, pressing against the wall and swallowing.

The motorcycle sputtered to a halt.

The echoes of its engine filled the clearing and died.

Jennifer inched carefully along the wall, ignoring Marysue's groping at her jacket. She listened, heard no footsteps, and held her breath as she poked her head around the corner.

Someone was standing behind the car, dressed in a heavy black leather jacket and a black helmet whose visor was dark, reflecting the trees around it and revealing nothing of the man who wore it.

She pulled back and shrugged at Marysue. Then she looked across the clearing and saw Lee and Conrad trying to sneak around the back of the cabin. Lee still had his makeshift club, and Conrad seemed to be holding a large rock in his left hand. When Lee saw her, he waved and motioned her to stay where she was.

If there's one, she thought, there have to be more.

The woods now took on a different look. Gone was the postcard effect, the peaceful sounds. Now they were filled with menace, and she couldn't help seeing movement behind every bush, every tree, and she even held her breath for a second when something splashed into the water and sent ripples to the shore.

She looked a second time and saw the man in black coming around the car, tugging at his helmet. And when it was off, she said, "Thank goodness!" so loudly and suddenly Marysue almost screamed.

Borden Overbrook grinned when he saw the quartet converging on him, and he tucked the helmet loosely under his arm.

"You scared us half to death," Marysue accused when they reached him.

"Sorry," he told her. "I just thought, after what Conrad told me, that it would be easier to use the bike than the car. I didn't mean to frighten you. As it is, I passed that sorry excuse for a road twice before I realized you'd turned in here. Brother, it sure is tucked away."

Lee stared at him sullenly, but Conrad, after tossing the rock into the bushes, told him what they had found— or what they hadn't found.

"Are you sure this is the place?" the instructor asked after he searched the near cabin on his own. "It doesn't look like anyone's been here for a hundred years."

"Sure am," he said. "She told me to go to the Witch's Eye, and this is it."

"What?" Jennifer said.

"Sure," Conrad said with a shrug. "Didn't you know that?"

W.E., Jennifer thought. Witch's Eye. That's what the woman meant on her list.

"Doesn't look like a witch's home to me," Overbrook muttered as he walked toward the small lake. "Looks like an old-fashioned fishing hole, in fact."

They trailed behind him, Lee at the rear with the club still in his hand.

"Oh, yeah," said Conrad. "It's the water, see?"

They followed his pointing finger.

To Jennifer it just looked like water, and she exchanged shrugs with Marysue.

"It's the reflection," the boy said when Overbrook asked him to explain. "They say that from up a tree, or on top of the hill, the lake is just like a big eye. And when a cloud passes over it, it looks like it's winking or closing." He slipped his hands into his jeans pockets and nodded toward the center. "You can't see it right now because of all that garbage floating around. But they say that's what happens."

"But why *Witch's* Eye?" Jennifer asked.

Conrad kicked at a stone and watched it bounce into the water. "Well . . . it's silly, really."

"Is it?" Overbrook asked turning to face him. "Why?"

Conrad hesitated, and Marysue poked him lightly in the small of the back. "Just tell us, okay? I don't want to stand around here until it gets dark."

Lee said nothing.

When Marysue prodded him again, Conrad relented, though not before he gave her an angry look.

"Well, my mother, she's from around here all her life, she says that there are some times when the water darkens just like a cloud is passing over. Except there isn't any cloud. It just goes dark. The story is that back before the Revolution, this is where the locals used to burn the people they thought were witches."

"Swell," Marysue muttered.

Conrad's smile was embarrassed. "They say the witches aren't really dead, though. Their bodies were tossed into the water, and they're trying to get back out."

"Wonderful," Marysue said, rolling her eyes heavenward. "Halloween is still two weeks away, you know. Couldn't you have saved that stuff for then?"

"Hey, c'mon," he protested. "It's only a story."

Overbrook looked around again, slowly, and crouched down by the water. He pulled off a glove and flicked a pebble at a lily pad. "A lot of people still believe it, though, right?"

"What?" Conrad put his hands on his hips and looked at Lee, who was still standing a few feet from the others. "No, of course they don't believe it."

"This place isn't used all that much."

Conrad started to laugh and stopped. "Because the fish are gone, that's why."

"I see."

"Well, they are!"

Jennifer stared at him in amazement. He believes it, she thought. Conrad, who practically has his own lab in the attic, believes this place is haunted.

She would have laughed if he hadn't seemed so anxious to drop the subject, and as they moved slowly back toward the cabins again, she could see why Mrs. Klopher would consider this area in her search for . . . whatever it was. The lake was far off the road around the back of Ballad Hill, the stories kept many of the locals away, and from the looks of the ground the teenagers didn't even use it as a place to party.

For all anyone knew, the Witch's Eye might not even have existed.

"Now what?" Lee said when they reached the cabin.

"You checked around?" Overbrook asked him. "You didn't see her?"

"No."

"Then I suggest we wait awhile." He pulled back his jacket sleeve to check his watch. "Let's give her an hour. The sun will set by then. If she's not back, we'll return to school."

"Then what?"

"I don't know, Lee. Okay?"

Jennifer frowned at the tone in Lee's voice, and she took his elbow to lead him away so that the others couldn't hear.

"Lee, what's the matter?" she asked.

He didn't look at her. He didn't answer.

"Lee, c'mon! You've been acting funny ever since he got here. What's going on?"

He looked away, toward the car, and back again. His eyes were narrowed and his jaw tight. "I don't trust him," he admitted finally.

"No kidding," she said and grinned when he looked at her in surprise. "When you're mad," she explained, "it isn't hard to tell what you're thinking."

"Oh, yeah?"

"Yeah," she said, mimicking his tough-guy voice. "Now lighten up, okay, and tell me why. I mean, he's trying to help us, isn't he? And didn't we agree he'd be the perfect one to have on our side?"

"I guess."

She stopped in front of him and stood close. "You guess? What does that mean?"

"Jenny, I just don't trust him, okay? I got a feeling.

"Feelings can be wrong," she said.

"I know. But it seems so . . . perfect, you know what I mean? All of a sudden, here he is, going along like he knew about this the whole time. He hasn't checked your story about the trustees, he hasn't seen one of the creatures, he accepts everything we say. It's . . . not right."

They started to walk again, past the cabin now, toward the treeline on the clearing's far side.

"He explained all that," she told him, watching her feet vanish and reappear in the carpet of leaves on the forest floor. "He's worried about Mrs. Klopher."

"I know, I know."

"But . . . ?"

"I told you, Jen. It's a feeling, that's all."

Suddenly Lee whirled around, club high, and Jennifer screamed when something bolted out of the brush right for her.

# Nine

LEE MANAGED TO PULL THE SWINGING CLUB ASIDE just in time to avoid hitting a tiny dark figure that had tripped over a rock and rolled onto its back with a muffled curse. A large black stocking cap was pulled back from its face, and Jennifer, who had thrown herself to one side, climbed slowly to her feet, too amazed to do anything but gape.

"Sorry," said Pauline Klopher flatly. "I tripped. Very clumsy."

The others had come running at Jennifer's startled cry, and they stared at the librarian as she hauled herself painfully to her feet and dusted clinging leaves from her heavy black clothing—sweater, trousers, and the cap pulled low over gray-streaked black hair knotted into a clumsy loose bun at the back of her neck.

She was small and thin, and her hands trembled violently as she tried to pluck a blade of grass from her sleeve.

"Pauline!" Borden said anxiously, taking her arms and holding her back so that he could see her. "Are you all right?"

"If that boy there doesn't brain me, I will be," she said, glaring at Lee, who still held his weapon.

She yanked off the cap and stuffed it into a hip pocket, and the light that fell on her face deepened the creases, made her large eyes seem more round, and touched her pale skin with a semblance of color.

"You weren't there," she snapped at Jennifer. "Yesterday you didn't come when I asked."

Jennifer, still shaking a little from the scare she'd gotten, couldn't do anything more than shake her head helplessly.

"It wasn't her fault," Borden said quietly. "She got the message late."

"How do you know about them?" Jennifer asked, suddenly finding her voice.

"For heaven's sake, girl, not here, not here," the woman said testily. She started back for the trees, stopped when she realized no one was following, and stood with her hands firmly on her hips. "Well? You going to stand there all night or are you coming?"

Lee and Jennifer looked at each other, looked at Conrad, who gave them an exaggerated shrug and plunged through the underbrush when Mrs. Klopher turned and started walking. Marysue rubbed her arms nervously, not moving until Overbrook tucked his helmet more securely under his arm and moved on; then she hurried after them. Her face when Jennifer saw it was bloodless and drawn.

"I . . . I could have killed her," Lee said hoarsely.

Jennifer took his hand.

"I could have brained her, the old fool."

They started into the trees, seeing that the others were following a narrow deer trail that wound around the brush and trunks toward the far side of the lake. It didn't take long before the clearing was left behind, and only an occasional glint of water to their left reassured them they hadn't gotten lost.

The only sound was the crackling of leaves crushed under their heels, the snap of twigs, and the whispers of the two adults in the lead.

Jennifer ducked beneath an overhanging bough and nearly tripped over a log fallen across the path. It was then that she realized the light was failing. When she looked up, she saw the sky darkening.

The air chilled.

The breeze died.

"This is crazy," Lee muttered.

Jennifer said nothing. Despite his misgivings, she wanted desperately to trust both Overbrook and Mrs. Klopher; if she couldn't, there was no one else—and if there was no one else, then she and her friends were truly lost.

It took them almost half an hour to reach their destination, a small clearing less than twenty feet across. It was so round, so empty of vegetation, that it couldn't have been natural, and even in the quickening twilight Jennifer could see that the trees opposite her were dying.

Pauline stood in the center, holding a flashlight and pointing at the bark peeling off a stand of white birch; then she bent down and picked up a branch, held it out to them, and nodded at brown leaves curling inward toward their stems.

"This is a maple," she said. "Or it used to be. It should be gold, or red." She tossed it aside in disgust. "Even the pines are dying."

"Acid rain," Marysue said, clinging to Conrad's arm as if afraid he would desert her. "Dr. Overbrook's told us all about it."

The librarian sniffed. "That right, Borden?"

"Well, sure," he said. "It's happening here, down in the Carolinas, over in New York . . . whole forests in Germany are dying because of it."

"That right?" she said again.

Puzzled, he looked hard at her. "If it isn't that, it's gypsy moths. Though . . ." He stared into the trees. "I don't see any signs of them here."

"I know," said Pauline. "And you won't, either."

Before any of them could answer, she was off again, leading them across the clearing and into the trees beyond. Another trail, this one somewhat wider than the first, and the ground began to slope upward.

Jennifer looked at Lee for an explanation, but he was too busy staring at the dead and dying trees, some still standing, others fallen as though they'd been snapped in half by a giant, the pith inside crumbling and gray. He shook his head and slapped his club at one tall stump, sending a cloud of dust into the still air.

She wanted to rush ahead and ask the woman what was going on, how she knew about the creatures, how she knew they knew, and why she was out here; she wanted to know about the ransacking of the apartment, and the reason for the woman's choice of clothes—as if she were engaged in a midnight commando operation.

They angled toward the center of the back of the hill, stopping only when they reached a second clearing, this one far more desolate than the one they had left behind. It was, Jennifer thought, as if some madman had taken cans of brown and gray paint and thrown them over everything.

Nothing, not even the grass, had been left alive.

"Must have been a heck of a fire," Conrad said as he knelt and poked at the dead grass. Then he frowned. "Funny . . ."

"What's funny, young man?" Pauline demanded gently.

He looked up at them. "I don't know. It looks burned, but there aren't any ashes."

"The rain would wash them away, dope," Marysue said.

"No. Some of it would stick around, packed like dirt. But I don't see—."

"And you won't," the librarian said.

"Mrs. Klopher, please," Jennifer said.

The light was almost too dim for her to see, the darkness building a wall around them, drawing the forest in to form a black, shifting cage.

Pauline nodded once. "You're right, Miss Field, please forgive me. You might say I've had a lot on my mind."

"Such as?" Overbrook asked.

"Such as the creatures these young people have been chasing for the past few weeks."

Jennifer closed her eyes in relief. "You *do* know," she said.

"Oh, yes, my dear. I do know indeed."

Before she began to explain, Pauline Klopher pulled a plastic garbage bag from under her sweater and directed the others to scoop up twigs, branches, grass, leaves, and samples of bark from the surrounding trees.

As they worked, she spoke.

And the more she spoke, the colder Jennifer grew.

She had been at Thaler more than twenty years, had seen teachers and students come and go, had seen the administration change hands more times than she wanted to remember. But when the former dean, John Innlake, had been forced from his position when Peter Dramon took over, she had wondered if there wasn't more than simple academic politics involved.

Things had been happening.

Odd things which, taken separately, meant nothing to anyone not looking for a connection.

She told them how it wasn't long after Dramon arrived that the trees there began dying. She knew because she spent much of her free time roaming the woods; it gave her peace, she said, and she enjoyed taking her camera with her to photograph what wildlife she came across. And when the trees began dying, the wildlife left for better pastures.

Those, she said, that weren't already dead.

She had thought, in the beginning, that a company was doing illegal dumping there—toxic wastes of one kind or another—but she found no evidence of it; then she had wondered if the destruction of the old science building and its hidden laboratory wasn't somehow connected—perhaps, she speculated, the experiments there had to do with something like pesticides.

"Being a librarian," she said as they headed back toward the lake, "is a wonderful excuse to get nosy. You can always say you're doing some research."

At the same time she began to hear stories from her friends in town, stories about prowlers and thieves the police never seemed to be able to find. She thought little of that until John Innlake was murdered shortly after Jennifer and Marysue had been sneaking around the library, looking for something to tell them about the school's history.

"You knew?" Jennifer asked, astonished.

"Esther Fine broke down and told me you had asked permission to stay when the library was closed. The next morning I found the books you had been looking through. And I've seen too much in my life, read too much history, not to be able to draw certain conclusions."

It was only four days before that she had seen her first creature.

Jennifer frowned and glanced around. The woods were getting noisy. She could hear, just behind them, something that sounded like an animal rushing through the brush.

None of the others, however, seemed to notice, and Overbrook questioned Mrs. Klopher, "You've seen one?"

They started moving then and returned to the first clearing at the base of the hill. It was too dark to see the trail now, and Mrs. Klopher pulled a small flashlight from one of her bulging pockets to guide them.

"I was walking," she said. "Down by the pool. A warm night, and I couldn't sleep. I heard noise and thought it was some of the girls sneaking around with their boy friends."

"The creature," Overbrook reminded her.

"Oh, yes."

She wiped a hand over her face slowly, and Jennifer saw how weary the woman was. She wanted to rush up and hold her arm—but knew that she would only be snapped at.

"I came face to face with two of them," she said, as if she were talking about coming across a pair of harmless dogs out for a night's prowling. "At first I thought they were in costume, practicing for Halloween. I was going to scold them. But when I approached them, they howled at me most convincingly and ran away."

None of them said anything for several long seconds.

Jennifer looked behind her—the noise again, closer.

"I saw another one the night before last. Outside the house, Borden. In the yard. I was walking by the window and happened to look out, and I saw one standing just beyond the light from the kitchen window downstairs.

"It was watching my room. It was watching me."

Marysue shivered violently, and the woman looked at her with a sad smile.

"Imagine how I felt," she said. "And you can imagine that I didn't get much sleep that night."

They walked into the cabin clearing, close enough together so that they could reach out and touch if they needed to. They wasted no time, but headed straight for the car.

"But I don't understand," Jennifer said. "Why didn't you tell someone?"

Pauline stopped and looked up at her. "Why didn't *you*, dear?"

"That's easy," Lee said. "We knew no one would believe us."

"And me? Who would believe an old woman like me, locked away year after year with her precious books? Dotty, they'd say. Too much time staring at pages, too much reading, too much imagination." She shook her head. "No, Mr. Fawkes, you young people aren't the only ones who have trouble with the grown-up world."

Jennifer looked quickly at Overbrook, remembering what he'd said to her in the kitchen the night before. Then she turned to the woman and said, "But why are they after you? You haven't done anything to them."

"Oh, yes, I have," she said. "I don't know where they're from, but I know why they're here."

# Ten

"LATER," PAULINE HAD SAID WHEN DEMANDS FOR information threatened to become babble. "Later."

Jennifer was now in the backseat, sitting on the edge so she could lean on Marysue's backrest, the better to hear over the whine and protest of the engine.

The twin boulders rose ahead of them and passed so close she expected to hear the shriek of metal scraping against them.

The headlights made the woodland night seem much darker, blotting out everything save what was trapped in their beams. And Conrad drove fast, which made the bumps seem higher, the depressions deeper, and more than once she thought she saw something running beside them, just beyond the trees, out there in the dark.

Each time she stared, it would be gone.

She remembered the noise and wondered.

"There's no time now," the old woman had snapped. "Let's get a move on. We'll talk later."

Then she had grabbed the half-filled garbage bag out of Zucco's hand and fairly leaped onto the back of Overbrook's motorcycle, waving to him impatiently to get the thing moving. When he offered her his helmet, she shook her head disdainfully and jammed her stocking cap on. In the dark she was nearly invisible.

"Our little band grows," Conrad said as he wrenched the wheel to avoid hitting a tree stump.

"Like Robin Hood's, right?" Lee said sourly.

"Oh, great," Marysue grumbled. "Some band. A few kids, one teacher, and a little old lady librarian who goes around dressed like she was fighting in World War Two. Great. I don't believe this, you know. I really don't. If my mama could see me now, she'd disown me."

The car lurched heavily to one side as it jounced over a rock; for a moment the headlights stabbed the woods, swung back again, and steadied on a thin plume of exhaust from Overbrook's bike, itself already vanished as the instructor raced toward the road.

Jennifer stared hard at the sweeping shadows, then told herself to stop—if there was anything there, anything trying to keep up, she wouldn't be able to see it anyway, at least not clearly; and if there wasn't anything, her imagination and nerves would create it and scare her.

She closed her eyes for a moment and wished she were home.

"Come on, Zucco, come on, keep up," Lee said tightly. "He's getting too far ahead."

"I'm trying, I'm trying, okay?" Conrad snapped without looking around. "This ain't a limo, you know. It'll probably die after this anyway."

Marysue slapped his arm. "Don't use that word."

"Sorry."

"Just don't use it."

Jennifer felt the tension like static electricity looking for a place to spark. And after the others quieted down, she held on to the back of her friend's seat and stared blindly through the windshield, trying not to think, trying not to wonder just what it was Mrs. Klopher knew.

Obviously, it had something to do with the materials they had gathered from the far clearing, but what? Was she trying to say that the aliens were the cause of acid rain, in spite of all the evidence to the contrary?

That was crazy.

But so was that night.

"There he is," Conrad muttered.

The bike glinted in the glow of the headlights, and it was a long, disturbing moment before Jennifer was able to separate the black of Mrs. Klopher's clothing from the black of Overbrook's jacket.

She shuddered.

It was almost as if they had grown together into one large creature on a demon-powered machine.

Then, abruptly, they were all on the highway. Overbrook waited for them on the shoulder, with Mrs. Klopher clinging to his back with one hand and the garbage bag with the other. Conrad pulled alongside, stopped, and rolled down the window.

"We'll meet in my apartment," the woman said. "Get there as fast as you can without killing yourselves."

Overbrook snapped up his visor, his face ghostly pale in the glow from the car's lights. "Too risky, Pauline," Jennifer heard him say. "If the police are there, they'll want to know where you've been all this time, and you'll be tied up with them for the rest of the night."

She thought for a moment, then shifted her grip on the bag. "I think, better the police than the wolves," Pauline said with a sour smile. "Let's go, son. Move this machine."

Overbrook shrugged, nodded to Conrad, and pulled out onto the road. Conrad followed close enough to keep the bike in his headlights.

"I don't get it," Lee said once they were up to speed. He raked a hand through his hair and looked around him in bewilderment.

"I know what you mean," Marysue agreed. "It's going so fast I can't think. I can hardly breathe."

An automobile passed them, heading in the other direction, its taillights, when Jennifer looked back, glowing like the eyes of a big cat. The image unnerved her, and she looked quickly away.

"Yeah," Lee said reluctantly. "But there's something else, and it's driving me nuts that I can't think of it."

This time it was Jennifer who understood. Through all of this, a question had been shouting at her from the back of her mind. It was as if she were listening to it from the far end of a long tunnel—by the time the words reached her they were jumbled. But the tone of it told her the message was urgent, which made it all the more frustrating because she couldn't understand.

The road began to curve then, following Ballad Hill's contour, and she watched, fascinated, as the motorcycle seemed to hang on the edge of the tarmac, following the rim only inches from the shoulder and the trees. She had never been on a motorcycle, and the thought of it terrified her.

A flare of brilliant white light filled the interior then, and Conrad muttered something as he glanced into the rearview mirror.

Marysue looked back and sneered at the automobile pulling up behind them, its bright lights on. "Idiot," she said. "It's a no-passing zone. What does he want us to do, fly?" She looked at Jennifer and grinned. "If I only had the T-bird, huh? I'd show that creep a thing or two."

The trailing car drew nearer, the rear window filling with light now as if it were coated.

"Slow down," Marysue said. "Maybe he'll go around."

But Conrad nodded toward the bike. "I don't want to lose them."

"You know where they're going. Please, Zucco, slow down before that guy kills us."

The car came nearer still, and Lee shaded his eyes against the glare as he tried to make out who it was behind them. Jennifer squirmed until she was almost kneeling on the seat and looked at him fearfully.

"Maybe it's the police."

He shook his head. "They like their red lights too much. At the rate we're going, we would've been pulled over a long time ago. The jerks."

"Maybe," Conrad said, "it's Rumbel."

"No. He's a jerk, but he's not that stupid."

Silence then.

Jennifer squinted, trying to make out the shape of the car, trying to see through the white light to the face of the driver. But she could make out nothing at all, and the car remained where it was, only a few feet from the bumper, matching their speed.

"Maybe they're friends of yours," she said to Lee. "Maybe it's a joke, huh?"

"Some friends," he grumbled. "Jerks. Drunks, probably."

Suddenly a horn blared, and Marysue uttered a short scream.

"It's okay," Lee said angrily. "He's just trying to scare us."

The horn blared again, and the light in the window faded as the car came close enough to hide its headlights.

"Lee," Jennifer whispered.

The road straightened, and Conrad stomped on the accelerator, trying to force the old car to a speed it could never reach. His knuckles were white, there was sweat on his forehead, and Jennifer saw his lips moving as if he were praying silently.

The red car whined.

Marysue shoved at the dashboard as if she could help the car go faster.

The horn sounded again.

"Why doesn't Mr. Overbrook help us?" Marysue asked then. "Can't he see what's happening?"

But the answer was obvious when Jennifer looked out the windshield—the motorcycle was gone. There was nothing ahead of them but the black stretch of the road.

Marysue looked too, but she only shook her head. "But he's gotta hear it, right? I mean, he's gotta hear that guy's horn, doesn't he?"

He does if he's listening, Jennifer thought. Unless, up ahead, there was someone else waiting for him, just as someone had been waiting for them.

"Oh, no," Conrad said fearfully when he checked the mirror again. "He's gonna—"

The car jumped forward sharply as it was nudged from behind, throwing Jennifer into the back of the seat ahead. The air was punched from her lungs, and she fell back, gasping, listening as Conrad shouted wordlessly while fighting to keep the steering wheel from slipping out of his grip. Marysue screamed and pressed herself against the door, looking back, looking ahead, shouting for Conrad to slow down, to stop.

The horn.

Lee's hands curled into helpless fists, and he pounded them against his thighs, against the seat, until Jennifer grabbed for his hand and he gripped hers tightly.

Again they were bumped, and the right wheels slid toward the edge of the road, kicking up pebbles and rattling them like machine guns against the undercarriage and the sides.

When they were struck a third time, almost lightly now, Jennifer felt as if she had suddenly become hollow—nothing inside her but a dull, shifting chill. Lee urged Conrad quietly to let his foot off the pedal.

The engine's whine settled lower.

The speedometer's red needle began to swing to the left.

And when the road arched into another curve, the trailing car fell back, white light once again filling Conrad's car.

"Drunk," Lee said a second time, though it was clear he didn't believe it.

Conrad blew his horn, twice, once, twice, trying to signal the bike.

"They're gone," Lee said, his voice hoarse.

Marysue, her face glistening with tears of fright, rolled down the window to gulp at the night air.

Then the car charged them again, striking the rear bumper on the left, drifting back, and striking it again.

Lee shouted and grabbed for Jennifer, who flung her arms around his shoulders.

The horn sounded.

The dark car charged.

Marysue closed her eyes, and Conrad lost control.

# Eleven

JENNIFER REMEMBERED LITTLE JUST AFTER THE CAR was struck.

Dimly she heard Marysue screaming in fear and anger, heard Conrad grunting as he struggled with the steering wheel, and heard the screech of the tires as they fought and failed to keep the vehicle on the road.

Then, for the longest moment, Jennifer was flying—completely weightless, with the silence broken only by a distant humming. When the moment ended, the world began to spin wildly, wrenching her out of Lee's protecting arms and throwing her against the side of the car, her head striking the window, her elbow slamming against the armrest.

There were lights bright enough to sting her eyes, lights of all colors that flared briefly like fireworks, and faded just as rapidly; there was the smell of burning rubber; there was the sound of metal creaking, wood snapping, and her own harsh breathing.

And voices.

Low, moaning voices, almost indistinguishable from the fierce pounding of her heart and the rush of blood in her ears. Finally she opened her eyes and found herself jammed into the corner, her elbow and head throbbing.

"I think I'm dead," she heard Marysue say shakily. Then, "Ow! Nuts, I guess I'm not."

With a hand pressed to her arm to calm the dull pain, Jennifer opened her eyes. She was alone in the back, and someone was moving past the door on her side. Slowly, anticipating pain from her injuries, she turned and saw Lee staring in at her fearfully and suddenly grinning like a fool when he saw she was all right.

He motioned to her to move away, and when she did he opened the door and helped her out.

"Easy," she said, relieved that the aches weren't so bad as she had feared. "My head's going to fall off, I think."

He laughed, but it was short.

"Will you look at that!" Conrad said dolefully. "It's gonna take forever and a half to fix this thing again. My mother's gonna have my head."

Jennifer accepted a handkerchief from Lee and wiped her face clear of the perspiration that drenched her. Then she looked at the car. They had evidently swung off the road sideways and, judging from the condition of the grassy shoulder, had spun around at least twice. The rear bumper was now crumpled into a deep V against a stout oak's trunk, and almost the entire driver's side was scoured with deep scrapes and dents.

Two of the tires were flat.

Steam hissed from under the hood.

One headlight was out, and the other aimed toward the tops of the trees.

Then, remembering what had caused the crash, Jennifer gave a start and looked toward the road, pushing herself against Lee until he patted her shoulder and said, "It's okay, they're gone, whoever they were. They kept on going."

Marysue and Conrad came over, and a quick check showed that none of them appeared to be seriously hurt. They were lucky. Had the dark car run them off a few yards farther on, or a few yards back, they would have slammed into trees much closer to the road.

"What if they come back?" Beauford asked.

"I doubt it," Lee said after a moment's thought. "I think they only wanted us out of the way for a while."

Jennifer, unable to take her eyes off Zucco's car, felt her knees give way, and Lee helped her sit on the ground.

"Just for a minute," she said weakly. "Just give me a minute and I'll be okay."

He said nothing, but kept his arm around her shoulders. Then he looked up at Conrad and said, "Your nose is bleeding."

"I'm fragile," the boy answered, taking a handkerchief from his hip pocket to stem the flow.

"Yeah," Marysue said. "Like an ox." Then she walked slowly around the car, shaking her head. "Y'know, Field, this is getting to be a habit."

Jennifer nodded. "Maybe we're charmed or something."

"Well, next time we're taking Lee's bicycle, right?"

"Right," Lee said and tried to stop Jennifer when she started to rise.

"It's okay," she insisted, looking into his eyes and liking what she saw there. "Really. We can't stay here all night. We have to get back to the school."

No one argued. They couldn't chance waiting for someone to come along and give them a lift, and they couldn't risk being picked up by the police. Not now. Explanations would have to be given, and most likely they would be taken into town, for a medical check as well as for further questioning about the accident.

Conrad forced the front passenger door open and pulled a flashlight from the glove compartment. Then he reached over and turned off the engine and the remaining headlight. A final pat on the steaming hood, and he led them off the shoulder.

A stiff breeze burst from the woods, making them all hunch their shoulders and close their jackets to their necks.

"This couldn't happen in summer, could it," Marysue complained as they followed the road around its curve. "No, of course not. It has to be practically the middle of the winter."

"It's only October," Lee told her. "You southern types are just too frail for real weather."

Their footsteps were loud, and the absence of street-lights made the forest all the darker for the tiny light they carried, the stars all that much brighter.

The moon wasn't full, yet it still outlined the road ahead, touched the tops of the near trees with hints of gray; and there were night-things in the air, sweeping and darting above them, the sound of their wings muffled, their occasional cries soft and touched with menace.

No one asked what they were.

No one looked up to find out.

Lee tried whistling, and stopped after three notes.

Marysue kicked a stone out of her way, and shivered when it slithered into the grass.

Jennifer massaged her elbow until the ache sub-sided, but she could do nothing about the dull throbbing that had erupted at the base of her skull. It was as if she were being repeatedly struck by a rubber hammer, and she couldn't help wincing when she probed the area and found a large lump. There was no blood, however, and she supposed she ought to be grateful for that, grateful indeed that she was alive at all.

Too stiff to run, they walked as fast as they could, the flashlight's beam jerking ahead of them.

"What I want to know," said Conrad finally, "is what Klopher was talking about back there. Does she really think those aliens cause acid rain?"

"No, I don't think so," Jennifer answered. "I think they're doing something else, something that caused all those trees to die."

"But what could that be?"

"Building a rocket ship to take them home," Beauford said.

"You watch too much TV," Conrad said. "You think they're making it out of logs, or pieces they're stealing from the school or something? Robbing hardware stores in Staines to get parts to take them to Alpha Centauri? Jeez, Marysue, c'mon. That's nuts."

"You got a better idea, genius?"

"Hey, don't snap at me," Conrad said. "This isn't my fault. Until I met you I was just a simple-minded, small-town Chinese-American boy looking forward to his declining years on the beaches in California."

Marysue hit him.

Conrad pulled her to him, hugged her, and handed her the flashlight. "Here," he said. "You're from Daniel Boone country, you lead the way for a change."

"I am not Daniel Boone," Marysue told him, sounding highly offended. "I am a society girl who has fallen into the wrong company, and you'd better remember it, pal."

Jennifer smiled at the banter, grateful they were still able to do it. But at the same time she knew it was partly an attempt to keep the dark at bay and partly a way to stop them from thinking about the close call they'd just had.

If only, she thought, their voices wouldn't sound so small out there in the middle of nowhere, still far enough from campus so that the lights didn't even brighten part of the sky.

Fifteen minutes later they stumbled to a halt.

They had just broken into a slow trot, four abreast, Lee on the inside, Conrad on the outside, when the flashlight jerked to the shoulder of the road and picked up a glimmering of metal.

"Hey," Marysue said when she saw it.

They slowed.

"Maybe it's just a beer can or something," Lee said unconvincingly.

"Too big," Conrad said reluctantly. "It looks . . . I think it's chrome." He muttered an oath under his breath and hurried to the shadowed verge, aiming the light down a short, slight slope free of trees and brush.

"Oh, no," Marysue gasped, hands pressed to her mouth, when the flashlight beam steadied and they all saw what was down there.

"Great," Conrad said. "Just great."

Lee said nothing, just touching Jennifer's arm in a signal to follow, and started down the slope, arms out for balance. Jennifer was right behind him, and the others followed quickly. When they reached the bottom they stood around Overbrook's overturned motorcycle, staring hopelessly, watching silently as the pale light drifted slowly over it.

"Maybe it's not his," Conrad said hopefully.

"It is," Jennifer told him. Her heart sank; her stomach felt hollow. "It is."

"Hey, guys, there's nothing wrong here," Lee said in quiet amazement, hunkering down to poke at the seat and the engine casing. Cautiously, he leaned over, checked the front and rear wheels, and looked up at Conrad. "There's nothing wrong with it. Nothing at all."

"You mean it didn't crash?"

"It doesn't look like it to me."

Jennifer moved back as he grabbed the handlebars and, with Conrad's help, lifted the machine upright. Once they had it steadied on the uneven ground, they checked it over, and, except for a few fresh scratches along the left side, they could find no damage at all.

Jennifer glanced up at the road, then at the trees at their back. She tried to imagine how this could have happened, then asked Conrad to play the light along the ground. As he did, she searched for signs of running, of breaking through the brush, anything that would indicate that Overbrook and Mrs. Klopher had simply abandoned the bike and run into the forest to escape their pursuers.

But after ten minutes of searching, she had to admit defeat.

"They must have forced them to stop," Marysue said in a small voice. When they all looked at her, she pointed to the road. "They got in front of them and stopped them, then got them in the car and slid the bike down here to get it out of the way. It would have taken too much time to hide it in the woods, so they just kicked it down or something."

"Makes sense," Conrad said. "I guess."

Jennifer, however, looked at Lee, and from the expression on his face knew he was thinking the same thing—from all they knew of the librarian, she wasn't about to do what she didn't want without a struggle. Forcing the bike over couldn't have been as easy as it sounded.

Only one thing gave her hope that the two adults were all right—both there and up on the shoulder she had seen no signs of any blood.

"I'm cold," Marysue said.

"All right," Lee said. "Does anyone know how to drive one of these things?"

Conrad shook his head, and Beauford lifted a palm.

When Jennifer gave him an apologetic shrug, he returned it with a grin and said, "Then we run on foot."

And before anyone could argue, he was charging up the slope to the road and was nearly ten yards along the blacktop before the others reacted and followed.

Jennifer, grimacing against the throbbing in her head, trailed, forcing herself to run because she didn't want to be left behind. She had no idea what Lee was up to, but the sooner they returned to the campus, the sooner they'd be able to rest, to think, to try to make sense of what had happened that night.

After that, she had no idea.

The only two people who believed in them were now gone, and once again they were on their own.

The road climbed, and Jennifer began panting, dropping farther behind; the only thing driving her on was the glow of campus lights. Soon, she told herself. It'll all be over soon.

Then the road leveled, and she could see the dark outlines of the pillars at the academy's entrance.

Lee was sprinting now, Conrad just behind, and Jennifer stretched her legs out, determined that nothing was going to keep her from the safety of her room.

And when the dizziness lifted the world on its side, when it seemed as if she were running along the stars to the moon, she still didn't stop until she felt herself falling.

# Twelve

THE ROOM, JENNIFER THOUGHT, WAS AWFULLY COLD. Someone must have left the window open. She shivered and felt a hand on her arm, felt something soft beneath her head, and she opened her eyes. Lee was staring down at her, frowning in concern, while Marysue and Conrad looked over his shoulder. It didn't take her long to realize she was lying on the road, her head in Lee's lap.

"I think . . ." She tried to sit up and didn't protest when he pressed a hand gently against her stomach. A deep inhalation, another, and a third, and she swallowed a surge of bile that rose into her throat. "I'm alive."

Lee's frown deepened.

"Trust me," she said, and this time she refused to allow him to keep her down. Tentatively, she pushed herself into a sitting position, held her breath, closed her eyes, and waited for the dizziness to overcome her again.

It didn't.

Her eyes fluttered open, and she looked over her shoulder. "Help me up," she said to Lee, who immediately jumped to his feet and gave her his hand. She stood carefully, not rushing it, and lay a gentle palm over the lump on her head. 'Too much too soon, that's all," she said and laughed at the look on Marysue's face. "Really! I'll be all right. Delayed reaction or something, that's all."

Lee stared at her for several seconds before nodding. "Okay, then let's get moving."

She dusted off her jeans and grimaced when Beauford took a slap at her back as she followed Lee between the pillars.

The campus was all alight, the lawns dark and rich looking; the air itself seemed to be softened by the white globes along the drive, dotted with window light from the buildings that sat in a crescent at the drive's upper curve. There were even lights in the Student Union, downstairs in the dining hall and upstairs in the library. One or two classrooms were in use, and to her right she could see the parking lot and three houses. All alight. All warm. All normal.

Then she looked behind her into the dark, and she shuddered.

"C'mon," Conrad said. "We've got to—"

"Go back," Jennifer said suddenly, without thinking.

Lee stopped as if he'd hit a glass wall. Marysue simply stared.

"It's where the answer is," Jennifer said. "You know that as well I do." She started walking toward her dorm, a feeling of urgency taking hold of her, though she didn't know why. She only knew that time had become vitally important, and the more they wasted, the more trouble Overbrook and Mrs. Klopher could be in.

The others fell in beside her. Lee, with a single encouraging look, told her that he too knew they had to move.

She spoke as she hurried on, looking straight ahead at the dorm growing before her as she neared it. "If whoever went through Mrs. Klopher's room found what he was looking for, there's no sense going there, right? And if he didn't, there's still no sense because we don't know what he was after.

"She said she knew what they were doing. And whatever that is, it has to do with the Witch's Eye. There's something back there, and we've got to find it. Now."

"But what about them?" Marysue demanded. "Aren't we going to call the police? I mean, they've been kidnapped, Jen!"

"And taken where?" she said. "We don't even know where to begin to look. And we'd definitely have a heck of a time trying to explain." She shrugged sadly. "It's the same old problem, and we don't have the time to find an answer."

"Her apartment," Conrad suggested. "Maybe they got away and they're waiting for us."

Jennifer didn't say anything. She headed for the porch as quickly as her legs would take her, climbed the steps, and looked down at them. Behind her, in the common room, she could hear someone laughing.

"If you want to check, go ahead," she said. "Maybe it's a good thing if you do. But don't you see? The answer isn't there anymore, not for us. We have to go back." She paused. "I have to go back. You guys can do what you want."

She turned and reached for the doorknob, and stopped when Lee asked her if they were going to walk or fly. She almost said, "We'll take the T-bird," until she remembered it was still in a Staines garage. She shook her head slowly. Walking would take them forever, but there was no one else they could trust, no one she could think of who might at least take them as far as the entrance road to the lake.

Then Marysue said, "Monica! We've forgotten all about her."

"Perfect," Conrad said.

Jennifer nodded quickly. "Okay. Lee, you stay here while Zucco checks the apartment. You can't come in anyway, not on a weeknight. We'll need sweaters, coats, gloves—"

"There is nobody in there," Conrad said, "who's my size."

"Don't be too sure, dear," Marysue told him with a grin. "Some of us are not quite as svelte as others."

The two girls burst through the door and raced up the stairs. Jennifer ran back to her room to grab sweaters and a coat, and she sent Marysue to do the same. Then, after checking to be sure there were no notes pushed under the door, and pulling on a ski sweater and a thick autumn jacket, she ran back into the hall and banged on Monica's door.

There was no answer.

The door was locked.

She groaned, kicked at the wall in frustration, and was about to head for the staircase when she heard someone singing in the shower room. With a silent prayer she ran down and poked her head in the door, recognizing the voice of Barbara O'Malley.

"Hey, O'Malley!" she called, peering through the cloud of steam that made the tiled room look filled with fog. She called again, and Barbara peered around the edge of a far stall.

"That you, Field?"

"Where's Monica?"

"I don't know. Swimming, I guess. The exercise, you know? She says it's good for her—to build up her strength."

Jennifer spat a curse and spun around in time to collide with Beauford. Quickly, she told her what Barbara had said, and Marysue volunteered to run down to the pool to find her.

Jennifer followed her more slowly, struggling against a faint dizziness she told herself was only a result of wearing too warm clothes in an overly warm building. And once she was on the porch again, the night air revived her. Conrad and Marysue were gone, and she handed a dark sweater to Lee and watched as he hurriedly slipped it on under his jacket.

"We're the same size," he said with a grin.

"Sure. It's probably stretched nine sizes already."

Then, with an exchange of glances, they moved off the porch, into the shadows between buildings.

"Jen, are you sure you know what you're doing?" he asked in a whisper.

"No," she admitted. "But I don't see what else we can do. And I'm tired of sitting around, waiting for something to happen. It's about time we did something, don't you think?"

"Sure," he said. "But . . ." He looked away. "They could be dead, you know." He looked back. "So could we."

She didn't say anything, only let him hold her. Suddenly, she silently wondered what she had done to deserve Lee, but she didn't want to question it further. He was there. He was on her side. And that was all that mattered.

Less than ten minutes passed before Marysue returned, complaining about the noise in the pool, explaining that she hadn't seen Monica though some of the girls had said she was there. "We're out of luck," she said glumly. "I guess we'll have to walk."

Jennifer swore. Then, with a sharp nod, she led the others into the light and down the drive toward the front gate, trying to keep her mind from running ahead of her. One step at a time, she cautioned herself. One step at a time.

Conrad ran into them as they got near the parking lot. As best as he could discover, Mrs. Klopher and Mr. Overbrook weren't in their rooms.

"Now what?" he asked, slipping on the deep blue sweater Marysue threw at him. "This thing is going to choke me."

"You'll thank me when you don't freeze," Beauford told him.

Suddenly Lee stared into the parking lot. He looked at Conrad, who followed his gaze to the cars. Conrad held up a hand. "You're crazy, Fawkes."

"What?" Jennifer said.

Lee grinned. "I am cold, my legs and feet are sore, and I am not going to walk all the way back to the lake."

Grabbing Jennifer's hand, he hurried across the band of grass between the drive and the lot and hesitated for a moment, scanning the cars gleaming under the lights. When he looked questioningly at Marysue, she pointed at the white Mercedes.

"No," Jennifer said. "Lee, you can't! She'll call the police! We'll get—"

"Quiet!" he ordered gently. "Don't worry. We'll be back before she knows it's gone."

"But why hers?"

Lee didn't answer. He tried the driver's door and held up a thumb when it opened. Without wasting a second, he ducked inside and vanished under the steering wheel, while Marysue, applauding without a sound, pushed Conrad into the back seat and Jennifer into the front. By the time the doors were closed, the engine was running.

And Jennifer almost screamed when someone tapped on her window. She rolled it down and squinted at the puzzled face of Martin Ellis.

"Young lady," the man said sternly, "are you aware that this is a weeknight?"

"Yes, sir," she said, wondering how she was able to talk at all.

Ellis rapped on the car with his knuckles. "The privilege of having a car on campus is not to be taken lightly. There are studies, you know. Tests. Term papers."

"Yes, sir," she said eagerly, before he could go on. "We're part of Dr. Overbrook's project on the Staines Valley ecology. That's why we have to go to the library in town. It has some material we need By tomorrow."

Ellis straightened. "And you put it off until the last minute, I take it."

She lowered her gaze. "Yes."

And thought, will you please *go away?*

Ellis shook his head and stepped back, opened his mouth as if he were going to say something more, and moved nimbly to one side when Lee suddenly pulled out of the parking space and headed for the drive.

Marysue groaned, and Conrad cleared his throat several times.

Lee didn't say a word, though he looked over at Jennifer and winked.

Jennifer, waiting for her breathing to return to normal and hoping that the man hadn't recognized her from the other night, watched him in the light of the dashboard. She didn't ask how Lee knew how to start a car without a key; there were other times when Lee had demonstrated other criminal skills. Instead, she squeezed down as far as she could in the soft leather seat and closed her eyes until she felt them racing down the highway.

They reached the turnoff without incident. There were no other cars on the road, and though the large sedan lurched heavily on the narrow side road, Lee managed to get them to the lake without using the brakes more than a handful of times.

He stopped just before the twin boulders, reached under the steering column, and the engine died without a sputter.

Then he turned to her and said, "Okay, boss, now what?"

# Thirteen

JENNIFER PULLED ON A PAIR OF WOOLEN GLOVES AND buttoned her coat to the collar. Marysue dug into her pockets and pulled out a flashlight that she handed over to Lee. Conrad still had his, and he tested it by sweeping the beam out the window and over the trees flanking the white car.

When he shut it off, their world turned to shades of black and gray.

The surface of the lake reflected the dim moonlight as if the water were made of silver foil; the trunks of the trees shimmered at the edges and cast formless shadows across the leaf-covered ground; the leafless branches were merely darker cracks in the dark sky, and they danced about stiffly when the wind came up over the top of the hill.

Even with the windows closed, Jennifer could hear the woods—rustling, crackling, whispering like a crone as she cast a dark spell.

Lee touched her knee with a finger, and she smiled at him nervously, pushed herself back against the door, and forced herself not to think of the time that was passing.

Rather, she looked through the windshield at the unnerving transformation of the Witch's Eye when the sun wasn't there. When the sun goes down, the old place dies and this one comes along.

Her eyes widened suddenly.

"Oh, no," she said hoarsely.

When Lee asked her what was wrong, she shook her head to keep him quiet and tried to recall what Overbrook had said in class. "And we're trying to make the earth into our own image of paradise."

"No," she said again; and the fear she had felt before was nothing at all compared to the fear she felt then.

"Jenny, come on," Lee said. "We can't sit here all night."

"Yes," she said. "Yes, you're right."

"So what now?" asked Marysue.

"The second clearing," she said. "That's where the worst of it is. And it wasn't fire that killed those plants, we know that. It wasn't fire, it wasn't toxic waste, it wasn't anything we could come up with in a million years."

You could be wrong, she told herself then, and prayed that she was.

And knew she wasn't.

She looked over the back of the seat to Conrad. "Those plants, the samples Mrs. Klopher had us take. I think I know what they died from. I think I know what Mrs. Klopher knows."

Conrad frowned at her. "But how?"

She told him what Overbrook had said and reminded him of how the leaves, the blades of grass, the bark on the trees had looked. "Think," she said. "What does it remind you of?"

"Jenny," Lee said almost angrily. "We haven't got time for games."

"This isn't a game," she snapped. "If I tell you, you'll think I'm crazy, or worse. You've got to come up with it yourselves. It's as much for me as for you, don't you see?"

"Yeah," Conrad said. "But I can think while I walk, Jen, and we've got to get moving."

Reluctantly, when Marysue and Lee agreed, she slid out of the car, gasping silently at the cold beneath the trees, whispering that she wanted them to get to the second clearing as quickly as they could, without sounding like the cavalry charging over the hill.

There was no avoiding the leaves, the twigs, the pieces of brittle bark strewn on the path. They could only try to minimize the noise as best they could. Following the beams of the flashlights, listening to the nightsounds erupting around them, trying not to look at the shadows overhead, the shadows at their heels, the shadows at their sides.

Lee picked up a length of branch for a club and passed it on to Conrad, who hefted it and nodded; Jennifer found one for herself and another for Lee, while Marysue found what looked like a stake whose point had been worn blunt by the weather.

Something ran through the trees above, showering them with pieces of leaves and a few twigs.

Jennifer stopped once to look back, staring into the dark and wishing the moon were brighter.

At the first clearing they paused while Conrad leaned over a gray piece of wood, turning it with his foot before grunting softly and moving on.

The wind picked up.

Jennifer looked up the slope of Ballad Hill and couldn't imagine that there was a road on the other side and the school just beyond it. What she saw was dark wilderness.

And it came to her that she was just as alien there as the aliens were on earth, perhaps more so because the aliens seemed to have made the dark their home.

She grew accustomed to the night noises of the woods, and she found herself listening for sounds that didn't belong—a stray echo, an odd snapping, a footstep that didn't match the ones she and her friends were taking.

They stopped at the edge of the second clearing, a gray and brown landscape. The only sound was their muffled, ragged breathing.

Then Conrad turned to Jennifer and said quietly, "Withered. They are withered."

She nodded and took hold of Lee's arm.

Marysue snatched a dead leaf from a bush and put it under the flashlight's beam. This one was brown, curled, brittle from the cold. She turned it over slowly before looking over her shoulder. "You were thinking about the bell jars, weren't you?"

Jennifer nodded again.

"Hold it," Lee said impatiently. "Wait a minute, okay? This isn't the same, guys. The plants in the lab died because they didn't have any air. They . . . what did Overbrook say? It was like they were strangled to death." He took the leaf from Marysue's fingers, bent down and picked up another, shone his own flashlight on them, then on the nearest patch of the ground, the nearest underbrush. "Nope. That can't happen."

But Jennifer wasn't listening.

As the dead white beams flashed around the clearing, she spotted what she thought was a continuation of the trail, down the slope to her left. With a brusque wave she hurried over to it, took Lee's arm when he reached her, and aimed the light through a break in the trees.

It was there—another narrow trail leading down and into the dark. She tried to picture the area in daylight but couldn't quite do it, couldn't quite remember how close the next hill was. But she knew that whatever the aliens were doing, they came from down there. Higher up would mean more exposure, a greater chance of being discovered.

She gave Lee a smile; he squeezed her hand.

*I'm scared*, she told him with a look.

*Me too*, he answered silently.

And they started down, much more slowly than they'd moved before, Lee holding the light straight down along his leg, illuminating only a foot or two ahead. Conrad switched his light off, and Jennifer heard what she thought was a whimper from Marysue.

There was only the moonlight.

And the wind.

And a large flat-topped boulder directly in their way that Lee scaled without a sound. He looked ahead and down. Jennifer watched his shadow-form, smiling to herself when the others pressed close to her. The warmth felt good, and so did the pressure of their arms against hers.

Then Lee scrambled down, panting, and said, "There's something moving down there."

The boulder was easily nine feet across, and without debate they switched off the lights and made their way to the top, lay prone on the cold stone, and followed Lee's pointing finger.

The trail, as far as they could tell in the moon's waning light, widened abruptly on the other side of the rock and led immediately into an open area several yards across. Though the trees were still thickly branched overhead, the underbrush had been cleared from this space. It looked perfectly normal, and would have been were it not for the moving shadow they saw on the far side. Back and forth it went, as if pacing or standing guard. They couldn't tell what it was—alien or human—because it stayed under the boughs of a line of high evergreens.

Jennifer strained until her eyes watered and still couldn't bring her night vision into clearer focus.

Conrad shifted.

Marysue inched back away from the edge.

Lee pulled up one leg as if he were going to leap. As he did, he dislodged a small shard of rock that rattled down the front and bounded into the brush. Instantly the shadow froze, and Jennifer held her breath.

Watching me, she thought. It's watching me, I know it.

Without stepping into the open, it moved toward them, one cautious step at a time, and she tightened her grip on her club, feeling a sliver of bark dig into her palm. She winced but made no sound, sensing the others getting ready as well. Four against one wasn't terrible odds, and she was less afraid of a fight than of seeing the creature.

It paused.

Lee sniffed.

Marysue's throat worked as she swallowed several times.

The wind gusted, lashing a brief hailstorm of debris into their faces, making them duck away, close their eyes, and look again quickly to see the shadow moving toward them still.

Lee reached over with his free hand and laid it briefly on Jennifer's shoulder. He squeezed it when a muffled grinding sound suddenly filled the air.

The shadow figure backed deeper into the trees and vanished.

Jennifer pushed away from the lip of the boulder, staring as a pool of dark shadow in the middle of the trail began to move slowly upward. Something was being raised from the ground, a tarpaulinlike covering. The grinding stopped, started again, and finally stopped as the oval cover was raised perpendicular to the ground.

There was no time to think.

They were staring into a gaping hole in the ground that the lifted cover had revealed. The next moment something was climbing out, swiftly, effortlessly, and then it was standing on the trail, stretching its arms over its head.

Wolf.

Wolf-creature.

It abruptly ended its unlimbering and pointed at the boulder.

And howled.

Lee grabbed Jennifer's arm and pulled her with him as he pushed himself off the rock and raced back up the trail. Conrad followed, pushing Marysue ahead of him.

Jennifer didn't need any encouragement. The baying of a hungry wolf on the scent of fresh prey was enough to spur her on, slapping at the branches that aimed for her face, grunting as she put out a hand to push Lee on.

They didn't hesitate when they reached the larger clearing and began their race back for the car. If they could just get to Monica's car in time, they'd be able to escape.

Only for a moment did Jennifer think about the librarian and her teacher, just long enough to decide that if they were still alive, they had to be down there, in the aliens' lair. But there was nothing she could do to help them then.

She ran, no longer trying to be silent, knowing it was futile, knowing the aliens knew more about this section of the woods than any of them.

She ran, and heard something moving up from the right.

Lee's head snapped around, snapped back, and he ran faster.

Through the smaller clearing they fled, following the dark tunnel of the trail, slipping, spinning.

The Witch's Eye glinted through a gap in the trees.

A few more steps, Jennifer told herself. Just a few more, Jen, and you'll be safe. It'll be all right.

They burst into the campsite with an audible gasp of relief, and Jennifer allowed herself a grin, a quick glance behind her. And it was too late when she turned toward the car and a wolf leaped on her from the cabin roof.

# Fourteen

JENNIFER SCREAMED WHEN THE CREATURE SLAMMED onto her, the club flying from her hand as she fell. Though her coat and sweater provided a cushion, the impact with the ground still knocked the air from her lungs, and she gasped, tears filling her eyes while the alien pulled back its upper lip, revealing long wet teeth. Jennifer thrashed, yelling, but the thing was too strong, and she wasn't able to get her legs or arms under her in order to push up.

There was a low growling in her ear as the creature grew ready to sink its teeth into her neck.

Then, suddenly, a blow, the alien grunted and fell off her, and she scrambled away on hands and knees, gasping. She rolled over, sat on the ground, and watched Lee and Conrad attacking it with their clubs.

On its back, its legs in the air, trying to regain its feet. The thud of contact made the creature's grunts of pain and anger nearly inaudible.

Jennifer staggered to her feet and swayed, her fear now replaced by a fierce rage that made her want to smash the thing into the ground. But she couldn't find her weapon, and all she could do was stumble toward the fight, watching in horror as the alien finally pushed itself upright and backed away toward the lake.

Then it howled, and for a moment everything froze.

The wind rattling through the trees was the only sound.

Lee swinging his club side to side was the only movement.

And in that brief moment, all she could think of was the dying that thing and its friends had caused, the terror and the nightmares, and she wanted to scream at it, to tear it apart with her bare hands.

But it ran.

The tableau broke suddenly, and the alien tried to run into the woods. Conrad jumped to block it, his club striking its waist and sending it reeling toward the lake.

Lee hit it from the other side, and Marysue was there, planting herself between it and Jennifer and raising her club high over her head.

It tried to charge, and Lee caught it on the shoulder.

It tried to run left, and Conrad slammed its leg just above the knee.

It howled and whirled and ran straight into the water.

The four ran to the shore and stopped, watching as the alien flailed toward the center of the Witch's Eye. It obviously did not know how to swim, but it had no other choice.

The creature made it almost to the middle before it vanished beneath the surface.

Jennifer grabbed Lee's arm and slumped against him when he put his arm around her waist.

The head appeared, mouth wide, eyes wide, its features clear for the first time since they'd spotted it.

It looked at them.

Green eyes.

And sank again.

The wind keened, and the water rippled, but the alien didn't surface again.

Lee was the first to drop his club, and the others followed as they backed away from the water, turned, and moved slowly toward the boulders and the car on the other side. They knew they ought to run, that there was still one more alien out there, but their legs were leaden, their arms numb, and Jennifer could feel Lee trembling beside her. Why hadn't the other creature attacked?

Perhaps it had decided to retreat.

Jennifer had had no idea what she or her friends were capable of, despite the fact that she had told Borden Overbrook that she would kill if she had to, to save her own life.

Now she knew she could do it if she were driven hard enough.

But she didn't like the knowledge.

Silently they climbed into the Mercedes, and Jennifer didn't even look when Lee hot-wired it again. The engine coughed and died. He tried again and succeeded, but didn't put his hands on the steering wheel. His face gleamed with perspiration, and it looked as if he were struggling to catch his breath.

Then he turned to her and said, "That thing almost killed you."

She only nodded. She didn't want to think about it. Then, "You guys saved my life."

Lee shuddered as if trying to shake off the memory of what had just happened, put the car in reverse, and started to back it toward the highway. Conrad and Marysue were silent, holding each other in the dark of the back seat until Jennifer turned around and smiled at them warmly.

"Thanks," she said.

"Just don't get any more ideas," Marysue told her, hugging Conrad more closely.

But he pulled her arms away with a rueful smile and shook his head. "We have to have more ideas," he said.

"Nope," Beauford said. "Not until I've moved to Brazil."

Jennifer sighed inwardly and looked over the hood of the car at the lake already being swallowed up by the bends in the road.

"I know," Conrad said, "what Jenny was talking about before. About the plants all dying."

Lee scowled in concentration, but his gaze flicked over at Zucco and back to the road. "Yeah," he said. "It's terraforming, right?"

"What's that?" Marysue asked.

Conrad patted her knee. "A concept in science fiction," he explained. "It's when the good guys—us earthling types—go to another planet and switch things around so that we're able to live there without support. You know, change the vegetation, the air—stuff like that."

"What does that have to do with . . ." Marysue could only finish by nodding in the lake's direction.

"That's what they're doing," he said. "Those plants were dead, Marysue, because they weren't getting enough air."

"But they were outside!"

"But they were, in effect, strangled."

Jennifer's hand moved unconsciously to her throat, her fingers massaging it gingerly.

Marysue frowned, thought, then sat forward with a gasp. "They . . . are you saying they're trying to change the air? Turn it into something they can breathe?"

"That's what it looks like, if we're right."

"But that means . . ."

Jennifer immediately pictured a device she had seen in the aliens' laboratory—something that looked much like the nose cone of a rocket, ten or twelve feet high, with a large porthole in the front through which she had caught her first glimpse of the creature without its human disguise. It was, she knew now, a chamber that permitted them to breathe their own atmosphere without the help of those patches they wore when they were on the outside.

One must be at the lair at Witch's Eye.

Who knew how many more there were?

They reached the highway and headed for the school. Lee drove slowly, constantly checking the side- and rearview mirrors. He had said nothing more, but Jennifer suspected that he was thinking about what Marysue hadn't spoken aloud—that the aliens were attempting to change the earth's atmosphere into one that better suited them.

And when that happened, the aliens would live, and everything and everyone else would die.

*If* they were right.

Only Mrs. Klopher knew for sure, and perhaps Borden Overbrook. But they were gone now, maybe forever, which left only her and her friends.

Riding through the night.

"I'm so scared," Marysue whispered.

Conrad hugged her tightly. "Take it easy," he said quietly. "It'll be all right once we know what to do next."

"I know," Lee said and glanced briefly at Jennifer. She nodded.

There was nothing else to do.

Not now.

After that night they had no more options.

She looked into the back and said, "We fight. We fight back.